Linda King
In
Silent Killer

Linda King
In
Silent Killer

Layne B Landis

authorHOUSE®

AuthorHouse™
1663 Liberty Drive
Bloomington, IN 47403
www.authorhouse.com
Phone: 1-800-839-8640

Published by AuthorHouse   10/01/2012

ISBN: 978-1-4772-7512-2 (sc)
ISBN: 978-1-4772-7511-5 (e)

Library of Congress Control Number: 2012918238

Dedication

I would like to dedicate this book to my parents. Richard and Joyce Landis with their love and understanding that I needed to be pushed in the right direction and to know when to say have some down time. With all my thanks and heart felt wish's. Thanks for the help. Also I would like to thank my Niece Jessica Brown for her help and encouragement. I hope you get your story in print one day. I really liked it! And for my two sisters for just being there when I needed you. For my twin brother with whom I could share my secrets with I hope one day you get everything you so richly deserve.

Any and all mistake in this book are mine. I have tried to be factual as much as possible. Even though this is a work of fiction; the facts makes the fantastic believable.

Introduction

In the world of Linda King her world will change forever sense her retirement for the Air Force. There she was a line staff officer and the commander of security police squadron. Her knowledge on the job was unparalleled and she could run a five mile race the fastest of any on her Military base. But questions about her personal life made her decide to retire from active duty. But certain forces have been watching her. One would want her to stay away the others wanted her back in the fold of justice. She chose justice and the plots start to slowly unfold. Somebody from her dark unknown past will work to stop her. Her own will to perform at her best to have justice served. Along the way she has revelations on what she can do and her own abilities.

Chapter One

Well another night shot to hell. Linda thought. That damn Frank has left the guardroom filled with cigarette smoke and the smell of burnt coffee. When will he learn you're not supposed to smoke inside? Ten minutes later and some air freshener and disinfectant, the air at least smelled a little better. She proceeded to fill out her shift log sheet and then got up and retrieved the magnetic proximity card and locked the room up.

Linda went on her first set of rounds in the empty Factory checking doors and putting the proximity card at the checkpoints. It was a boring routine but the client contact wanted them to do it. She returned to the guardroom after she was done and put on a pot of water to boil to make some tea.

She opened the newspaper she had bought before she came in and looked at the comics and then the help wanted ads. She fixed her green tea, poured a mug of tea, and set it down. Linda thought! I need a different job this one is a dead end. That damn Frank will never promote me while I am here; he cannot see anything but my tits.

Here she is a retired member of the Air Force, an Officer at that and this was the best that agency could find. Well she was still in the best shape of her life she ran 4 to 5 miles a day and worked out for one an half hours on the weight machine every day and she had a body that her supervisor called Hot! She was five foot eight inches tall and weighed right at one hundred and forty pounds. She was all muscle.

1

She was also well endowed with a rather large chest. The size was a thirty six D's and her hips were narrow to make her look somewhat top heavy. She also had very black hair that was long and straight and it went down to the middle of her back.

But Linda did not mind how she looked, she never considered herself really that good looking of a lady.

While she was in the Air Force she was training to be in the security police. Her mentor, friend, and dorm roommate was the same person her name was Jenny Long. Linda admired Jenny for her wealth of knowledge and her patience with the young Linda. She went in the Air Force at the age of nineteen. She learned her job well and soon was getting recognized for her efforts and her body by some of the others. But she rebuffed all their advances. She had a very bad experience when she was twelve years old; her foster father raped Linda. The lucky part was she did not get pregnant, she and her foster mother moved out of town after the trial was over and that was when Linda decided to never have sex with a man never again. She would only be with girls.

Linda soon learned in the Air Force there was a very strict don't ask do not tell policy of the whole gay/lesbian ordeals. She kept her mouth shut and did not make any advances on anybody. Until one night her roommate came back to the dorm room and Linda had just got back from the base gym and was wearing those very thin short Lycra shorts and a Lycra Crop top. Jenny came in and Linda was wiping the sweat away and saw Jenny was really upset. She asked her why the sad eyes Jen. Jenny just pulls out a letter from her pocket and says read this.

It is a dear Jane letter from her Husband Stationed in Germany. He says he wants a divorce because he has meet another woman and wants to marry her as fast as possible. Linda's gets a really pissed look and then realizes there is nothing she can do. She says Jen I can only say I am sorry to hear that. At that point Jen starts to let loose with the water works and she cannot stop crying. Linda kneels down on the floor next to the chair, puts her arms around her, and just holds her tight. After a while Jenny stops crying with a lot of soothing words from Linda and Jenny says could you take a shower please I really appreciate your help but you stink my friend. All right Jenny you could use one to. So Linda strips naked and so does Jenny and they wrap those big thick bath sheets around themselves and walk to the gang showers. They get there and there are several other girls in there showering or getting dressed or putting on make-up.

Linda hangs up her towel, gets in the shower, and gets it as hot as she can and Jenny gets in the stall next to her. When they are done they get dried off and go back to their room and finish with their hair. Linda puts on plain white panties and a very large Colts Football Jersey. Jenny has on her Pajamas and she starts to cry again. Linda said come over here and sit down with me. I will hold you tonight. So Jenny lay down on Linda's bed and Linda got in beside her and held her most of the night as a friend should.

A couple of months later Jenny was in Linda's bed a lot being held and Jenny was also holding on to Linda as well. They had become lovers. It just sort of happened. Neither one of them was looking to have the love affair.

Jenny's divorce had gone through and she was feeling on top of the world. But as life would have it. The Military gave Jenny new orders to England. Linda was very happy for her and said now my dear friend you know as well as I do that you have to be careful who you ask if you're a lesbian or not. But do not worry about me. I have enjoyed our time together; I would not change it for anything. Jenny replies! I feel the same way says Linda.

You helped me through a very bad time and I have known love again. I will always love you Linda I hope you do well in your career. On their last day together they Kissed in there room in private and said their good-byes and promised to e-mail each other as much as possible.

Well the years were kind to Linda she started to attend college and went for and got a full degree in Business Management. She then applied for and received her appointment to Officer Training School. She was to become an Officer for the Security Police.

She always heard from her dear friend Jenny Long and she always replied back in her e-mails never letting on that she was still a lesbian. Jenny had found out the Woman that her ex-husband married was a complete bitch and he left her and wanted his old wife back. She told him to piss off I never want to hear from you ever again.

Several years later Jenny was then caught with another woman. Jenny had been become a lover with the Base Commandeers wife and he did not want a big stink about it so she was asked to leave the Air Force. He got her an honorable discharge and a retirement.

The OSI asked Jenny who else she had been with and she said that she had been with no others. But the OSI did interview Linda and several of her roommates and friends she had throughout her air force career but she said nothing. She was a Major now and did not want to ruin her career.

Then a several years later she caught up with Jenny at a nudist resort in Jamaica and both caught up on old times. But Jenny says it was the base commandeers wife I was with. That is why I was asked to retire and not booted out. It would have made a big stink. That would have been something to see. Well my dear friend I have done well. I went on and I have become A Lt.Col in the Air Force. But they are playing the politics really hard. I am going to tough it out until I have my twenty years in and retire. With my ratings I should be able to last very well until then. I can take a guy I know to all those functions they want us to attend. He will not mind. He is a civilian and a decent friend to me. They are wondering why I am still single. I never told them! My foster father raped me when I was twelve years old.

I had grown up in Nevada. I am half Indian and half Russian decent. He saw what I was growing up as a very beautiful young woman and wanted that. I vowed to never be with another guy ever and I was an orphan. I love my foster mother a lot and she loves me. But she does not know about what I have planned. I plan on retiring at twenty years and seeing what else I can do.

Chapter Two

So later that day Linda and Jenny, both lay in a bed! They made love for old time's sake. It was still nice Linda; you were always the better one of us. You are good as always my friend! Well after today my leave ends and I have to be back on duty. In fact I am the Security Police Commandeer and I have to see the base commander later on. Then when the time comes I will put in my papers to retire. When the time is right give me a call some time and we will do lunch. If I do not have a dead end job that is.

Present day

Linda turns the page of the help wanted ads and looks at the security company ads. She sees her company in there and another one. Both very low paying jobs!

Then one catches her eye. It says Private Investigator Wanted Prior Military experience a bonus must have a P.I's License. Send resume and how to get a hold of you and best time. She writes the e-mail address down and the 1-800 phone numbers as well, pay is good with some Gov't contracts. She says to herself I like that. She closes up the paper, finishes up the paper work, and drinks another cup of green tea and does one more security patrol. When her relief got in, she is whistling a happy tune and waltzes out the door.

She drives home in her four-wheel drive pick-up truck and walks in her apt door and is greeted by her cat Jake. He is sitting on the end table next to the door as she comes in. He purrs very loudly, she looks at his food and water dish as sees they still have food and water in them. She closed and locks the door and walks to the bedroom and gets out of her uniform and throws it in the hamper. Next the bra and panties and she puts on a pair of Lycra running shorts and a Lycra crop top. Then she sits down in front of her computer and sends e-mail to the e-mail address she got from the P.I. and she attaches her resume and other info then she puts on her running shoes. Kisses her cat Jake good bye and steps out and locks the door and walks to parking lot and starts to stretch and warm up. At her age of forty now she needs to be careful.

So she warms up and stretches a lot for about a half an hour. Then she stands up and starts to do a five-mile run today. A little while later after the five miles has been run as fast as she can go? She walks until she cools down. The back to the apt and she kisses Jake again and strips naked in her bathroom and takes a very scalding hot shower. Then she dries off and climbs into bed naked like she has always done and goes to sleep with her hand on her customize colt .45 automatic pistol.

She woke up about 5 p.m. That evening with the covers thrown off of her again and Jake sleeping between her thirty six D's sized chest. She scratched his head and said wake up sleepy head I need to get up. He crawls off of Linda who is still naked and she gets up and goes to the Kitchen and gets a couple of hard boiled eggs and a hand full of carrots and a glass of Orange juice and fires up her PC again and looks for any new e-mail.

Her special sound chimes in of a machine gun going off and she sees she has a reply from the P.I. Guy. It reads! I love the resume. We have all ready done a preliminary background check on you and you come highly rated by all of your former commanders. I would like to meet with you. Please call this number and I will answer. Alex!

Well she thought I might as well. She picks up her cell phone and dials the number. It is answered on the second ring and the male voice on that end says hello Alex here! Hello Alex My name is Linda King I sent you my resume this morning.

Yes thank you for returning my call. You meet all the qualifications. All I need is two things! I need to meet you, and to finish up the background check. You understand that could take another 3-5 days. Yes. When did you want to meet?

Well I am off tonight but I need to do my work out then I can get ready say 8:30. Where do you want to meet? He says how's about Outback steak house. I will even pick up the tab. Oh that is thoughtful thanks! All right 8:30 sharp. She hangs up the phone, and asks herself what I should wear. Well first things first. I hit the gym.

She gets on her very tight compression full leg pants and a sports bra and a crop top with that and her jogging shoes with a very wide weight belt. She heads over to the gym, does a good warm up, and proceeds to hit the weights heavy. About an hour later she heads back to her apt and gets in a scalding shower and gets all cleaned up.

After the shower she wraps her hair in a towel, gets all dried off, and she puts on minimal make-up to accent her wrap around floral print dress. Her legs are well tanned so she wears no hose and nice shoes that are sure to make her feet groan in pain, but they really show off her legs well. Under the dress she has a sports bra on and her hair cascades down her back.

She gets to the restaurant and she is really starving about now. She tells the greeters that she is expected at a table with Alex. They say yes please come this way. They get there and there is a man who is in his late fifty's with gray hair and a slight paunch. He has a beer on the table. He stands and says wow your Linda huh! She replies! Yea that's me. You must be Alex.

Please sit down. Waiter! Please have another beer brought here for me and what would you have. I will have one as well. The waiter asks would you like to order now. Alex says I could, how about you Linda. She says I would like the 14 oz. Sirloin with a salad and an ear of corn. Alex orders a Strip steak with a baked potato and a small dish of steamed corn.

So Linda he asks! Why do you what to work for us? Well Alex as she sips her ice-cold beer. I need to get away from my dead end job. I need something with a challenge. My supervisor does not like me very much. He cannot see beyond my tits. Yea we got that from him and we knew about his assessment so we called your area manager and found out you are one of the best there. Always on time and reports are filled out correctly. I do try my best. As a Lt.Col and a Commander in the Security police field I had to have my shit together, as they would say.

That was what your last commandeer said! That you had your shit together! You could have gone on and made full Colonel within a couple more years. Well Alex here is the little kicker. There was a lot of politics and too many questions were getting asked.

I suppose you have done a little bit in your research all ready I have a friend who was asked to leave the Air Force because she was a Lesbian.

Yes we know about that and we know you are a known Nudist. We do not care about that! We have surmised that sense you have known Jenny for all these years that you were her first love! Linda thought about the reply on this. Then said! Yes I was her first and she was my first. I have been a lesbian ever sense my foster father raped me when I was twelve years old.

Alex got a shocked look on his face and said I am sorry to hear that, that is something we did not find that out. Do not be sorry that bastard got what he deserved. He was killed in prison two years later when they found out he had raped a girl who was only twelve years old. The prison officials called it prison justice.

Well I am glad that is out in the open. Me too Linda Replied! I would really love to do this P.I. work for you. But what would it entail. Well like I said in the ad I have several Govt. contracts and I get private ones as well. You would fit the bill for several of them. One is you

8

would go in a strip joint and work there to bust up prostitution ring. A strip joint, you mean taking off my clothing full nude?

Yes that it the one stipulation is the owner says it has to be believable. I do not have any of my girls that work for me that are as good looking and willing to go full nude. You are a 2nd degree black belt in Tae Qwon Do and a nudist as well. Well you are right on those accounts. I am not ashamed of my body. My mother and I have been Nudists for many years,

There meals arrive and they talk more and soon Alex says if the reports come back good then you will be hired as of that minute. The Security Company you work for will need a new replacement. Linda Replies! I would love to do this. Even the stripping job sounds like it could be fun. Would I get to keep the wages I earn under cover and the tips?

Sure just as long as you report them. Tell you what; you're off tomorrow as well. Yes I am she replies! Come to my office, he hands his card with his address on it and it is right down town. She puts it her breast pocket. They finish the dinner and she shakes his hand and says I hope we have a long and friendly working relationship. She walks out to her truck and drives home. She gets home, gets out of her cloths, puts on her Colts Football Jersey, panties, and sits in her chair with a bowl of popcorn, and watches movie's with Jake her cat on her legs watching with her. Then around 4 a.m. in the morning she gets up and stretches, goes to the bedroom and strips and gets in bed and goes to sleep very fast.

Chapter Three

$\mathcal{L}$inda wakes up that next morning with the phone ringing at eight a.m. She answers very sleepily and Alex is calling back. He says morning sunshine. Morning to you to sir she replies! What did I wake you up? Yes Sir, falling into her old routine of calling everybody Sir or Mame even if she out ranked them.

Well Linda if you want the job it is yours as of now! All you have to do is call your company and tell them you quit. Well Sir! Is this a two week state right? Well he replied I have some pull you will not need to. Just go down there and turn in your uniforms, meet here at my office tonight at 7 p.m., and wear something really sexy. All right Alex I will do. By seven ok!

Shit! I have not even slept three and one half hours yet. She sets her alarm for 11 a.m. and falls back asleep. At 11 she gets up, slaps the alarm off, gathers up her uniforms, and makes sure she has all of the pieces. She puts on a black faded jeans and combat boots with a white sleeveless tank top that is tight. She gets on her Truck and goes to her security office. She gets inside, talks to her area manager, and tells her she has gotten a better job. She says yes we got the request from one of our V P's to let you go without a two week wait.

You must be working for some people now who have that kind of pull. Well I do not know about that I am just going to be a Private investigator. Well good luck Linda I wish we had more like you. Well if that asshole Frank would have ever looked beyond my chest, he would have seen a good security supervisor. Rest assured he is being looked at she replies! She left that office and went to several thrift stores that day and found a couple of good costumes for stripping. She went home, did a five-mile run, and worked out in the weight room for one, and half-hours. Then cleaned up and put on denim mini skirt with white panties, and the stiletto heels shoes she got and a men's blue and white cotton flannel shirt, she tied off to just below her breasts. She drove down town with her pistol and two spare clips in her bag and arrived at Alex's office 30 minutes early. She parked and walked in and the receptionist asked who you are. Linda replies.

Alex just hired me this morning. Oh yea you're the one doing the stripping job. You look great by the way just call me Vie. I am here almost all the time. Here I filled out as much as I could on your paper work. Sit down here with me and we can finish it fast. Linda really liked how Vie worked. Quick and efficient and with such spunk she could see Alex must really rely on her. She looks to be in her late fifties with silver gray hair. She looked to be in excellent shape with slim hips a nice shape overall. Alex comes out when there almost done and says wow you still look great and dare I say like a stripper. Linda replies why thank you Alex. I use to bust a lot of young airman coming out of strip joints when I first went in the service. I would talk to a lot of the ladies who worked there. Some were very nice ladies some were not. I got a lot of advice from them on how to dress and the way they groomed themselves. Well you will work an 8-hour shift tonight, I asked, and they said it was full nude on your third act. You will also have to perform chair dances there as well. But just gather any intelligence on the prostitution ring. It is believed the bartender runs it with several of the girls in there. He will want to get his claws in you as well because of your looks alone. Well I am packing! I have my weapon with me, my license to carry. Oh and you must wear these earrings they are very tiny radio transmitters and with a 2000 foot range. We will have an agent within that range recording everything. All right Linda! Remember you are Toni Reynolds for the duration there. Got in Toni Reynolds Linda replies! Well I have a couple of more outfits in the truck. All right then get on down there.

The first night went well, the bartender leered at her a couple of times but a couple of the girls told her to throw a drink in his face, just make sure it is one of the drinks the customers buys for us. They are really watered down and the boss will not get upset about it.

She had six whole sets to do that evening and a free meal. She loved the thrill of the dancing and the stripping off of her clothing, what little there was. The meal was two large hamburger patties cooked medium well and some vegetables. She was trying to stay lean. Before the night was over she overheard one of the girls saying some about her that she would be a good one to add to the harem as she called it. She memorized the girl's name and went home. There she cleaned up and sent her friend Jenny an e-mail telling her she had a fascinating new job but she could not talk about it just yet. With it being sensitive and all. Talk to you soon! Linda! She sent it, striped off her clothing, and went to bed with Jake sleeping right next to her.

That morning she woke up as usual with Jake on her chest. She got him off, gets up, goes to the kitchen, and makes breakfast. A couple eggs and toast and juice and a hand full of carrots. She sits in front of her PC eating and gets the news of the world. She does not see much but what she does see is the threat rating for homeland security has been raised by one level. She shuts it down seeing that Jenny has not replied yet. Then she gets dressed for a run then the weight room. About 3 hours later. Linda gets back to her apt. She goes in and scratches Jake behind his ears and fills his water and food bowls again. Then she strips and gets in the scalding hot shower and cleans up. She then puts on her jeans and sneakers and her favorite colts jersey and grabs her bag and goes done to the office to tell Alex that she has found out damn little so far.

Later on that week after she had her first day off from the Strip club! Linda is in the office all day with other P.I.'s getting some training. On surveillance! Alex even buys lunch for everybody. She also helps out with a bust with the police with two other P.I.'s there as well Alex. It seems Alex has some pull with the police and the State police. The next night she is back at the club and about half way through the night when she is on her third act when she has taken all of her clothes off.

She sees the Bartender named Mike comes over with a piece of paper in his hand. She sees him take all of her cloths and puts the paper down on the stage where her clothes were. After the last of the five songs is done she gets the note and reads it. It says come to the bar; ask for Mike to get your clothing back.

She walks over to the bar still in her 6-inch tall spike heel stiletto shoes and naked. She stands they're looking defiant and ask where my cloths are at! Mike answers her; he says I will give you your cloths back on one condition. What's that Linda replies! That after you get dressed you come back her to the bar and we talk for a few minutes. All right she replies I will be back in ten minutes. She goes back and gets cleaned up a little wiping the sweat off and putting baby power on her body. Then she puts on a white skintight mini dress that is really stretchy It hugs her body like a second skin and she puts on a pair of white silk panties and the same 6-inch tall spike heel stiletto shoes. She goes to the bar and Mike reaches back and pours her a double shot of Johnny Walker Blue Label scotch and sets it in front of her. She says that is not our regular drink won't I get in trouble with that. No the boss is away and it has been paid for. Ok so what is on your mind Mike? Well Toni you are really one of the hottest looking ladies out there on the dance stage. Well thank you Mike! That's not all, the way you are dressed now is making me sweat a little and I am seeing naked girls all the time. Again thanks Mike. So what does this have to do with me?

You are perceptive Toni I will give that. I have a business opportunity for you. Oh! What is that Linda asks? You would make about one hundred dollars for one half-hours work at first. Linda replies wow that's some good pay what do I have to do jump out of a cake naked and sing happy birthday or something like that. No Nothing like that. You would be one of my girls! One of your girls! What do you mean Linda asks. Well you would take a man to a hotel room and have sex with him for one half-hour. Or longer if he pays me more! So Linda asks! You're saying I would be a Hooker for you. Yes! You would be a Prostitute for me. Linda says to herself! Bingo we have him. I am so glad these earrings have that 2000-foot range. All right Mike I am in. I need the money really bad. Well tomorrow night will be your first trick. You will meet him at midnight. But I am working here at midnight. Do not worry the time your gone will be covered. Also you will have to possibly do a trick after a shift or before and on your days off, a couple of times. Plus the better you get at it. The more you will make. Linda feels disgusted inside but she also knows that Mike will get his day in court and she will be there to help him along to jail.

Later she is sitting with a young man that is in the army and feeling a little bit guilty that she could not have stayed in herself. So she cheers this guy up and knows he does not have much money. So she slips him two twenty-dollar bills and whispers in his ear to ask the waitress to come over and buy the five-song chair dance. I will even go full nude for you on all the songs. So sit back and enjoy. The next dancer gets up on stage; Linda and the young army private have moved farther back so as to not distract the many on lookers to the stage show. There are some people back here. But Linda does see the three people sitting at the table behind them. She begins her dance like all the dancers do with all her clothing on then she peels her dress off standing there fully naked.

That was when she actually heard a few words of a language she would never thought to hear here. First there was German, which she spoke decently well from her time in Germany, and then there was Arabic as well. She almost lost her composure when she heard the phrase 20 million dollars In German and VX nerve gas and when can it be delivered and it is guaranteed to be deadly. She moved around to the front of the young man, climbed on his lap, and made a show of it but at the same time she did a quick study of the three faces at that table. One was most definitely of German or European stock and the other two had the Swarthy look and the long beards of one's she saw in Saudi Arabia.

She maintained her composure through all this and she did hear in German from the two. Why have you brought us here to this western decadence where woman parade around without clothing and cavort sexually? Because I enjoy it the other man said! Now let's get out of here. They get up and leave and Linda finishes her five dances, fully naked she kisses the young man on the cheek and a hug, and she says be careful over they're all right. Yes Mame he replies!

She walks back to the dressing room, gets her cell phone, and sends a quick text message to Alex telling him what she heard. She will get off at 4 a.m. She turns her cell phone off, and gets dressed again, then goes back out, and finishes her shift with little else happening. But she does learn whom several of the girls names are that are working as hookers for Mike in his little prostitute ring.

She walks out of the club that night with her hand in her bag on her gun and gets in her truck. After she has turned the corner she places a call to Alex and says Morning sunshine I am sorry to wake you but did you see my text message I sent? Of course not silly girl Linda says you were asleep! Then another voice is heard and Linda knows that voice is Vie's. She says morning Vie I am sorry I woke you both up but I feel this is an emergency, a big one Alex! Can you talk about it on the phone he asks? No I am afraid the phone has too many ears on it. All right meet me at the office in 30 minutes and bring some coffee for Vie, yourself, and me. Linda arrives there right at 30 minutes later just as both Alex and Vie are unlocking the office. Linda helps them and brings in the three large black coffees. Well this piece of info is secondary at the moment but we should have the evidence on tape for the prostitution ring. That is great Linda but you look worried. I do not like that look on a Military officer. Your right I overheard something disturbing while I was working in the club a conversation with three people.

With them speaking German! Which I know well enough to had a conversation. Well enough, I over heard them say 20 million dollars and VX nerve gas and can be delivered and is guaranteed to be deadly. Two of the men were of Middle Eastern descent and the third was German or European stock. If I had a police sketch artist right now I could give a good likeness of the three. All right Linda you have a very valid point and this will get very sticky. Vie dear I need to make some phone calls to my contacts and my people.

It is time we ask Linda here to join the team. What team is that Alex? Oh a Team like no other. We here in this office are all full federal agents but we are also Special Investigators with the Justice Dept. You're a Federal agent Alex? Yes and the paperwork has gone through to have you become one of us as well. But Alex I am a known Lesbian. The Govt. does not really like us that well. My dear they do not have to know. I never told anybody. Now you will have to be working at the club for a while more to see if you can get more intelligence on these guys and we will be working on our end. Vie will be your liaison at the club. I have been working on getting a bartender's job there. Just make sure you water my drinks down all right Vie. You got it Linda!

Alex went in and made several phone calls and by the time morning rolled around it was all set that Linda was now a full agent. A couple of more agents came in and got there briefing and the police artist came in, Linda had them draw the likeness of all three. They said they would put these through to Langley and Interpol to see what comes up. But we need more intelligence on this. Also by the time you show up for work tomorrow night the bartender Mike and the ones you have identified will be under lock with no key in site for a very long time. That's good I do not want them to get out and make me as the one who ratted on them. She goes home and does a five-mile run and an hour and a half weight room session. Showers and goes to bed as usual except this time she dreams of that federal badge she now has.

Chapter Four

That next morning Linda got up from bed and fixed breakfast and fired up her PC and she saw she had e-mail from Jenny. She opened it and it read. Why I am very happy for you my dearest friend, it sounds like you have a good change happening to you. The newest thing in my life is that Base commandeers wife left him and she has moved in with me. We are both very happy at the moment.

My dog whom I have named after you is doing well She loves to play all the time. Let me know what you can about your new job I want to know what my best friend is doing these days. Love Jenny!

Linda wipes a tear from her eye wishing she did not have to deceive her friend. But duty calls as she so often has said. She gets dressed for a morning run and heavy weight work out and does a long stretch and warm up. Then her badge and joggers bag around her waist and puts her Customized colt .45 in it with two full clips. Sense she was a full agent now she has to be armed at all times unless undercover.

Undercover at her present assignment, it is hard to hide a pistol when you wear just about nothing in the club.

She does close to six miles and then the weight room with heavy weights. She wants a bit more definition in her arms. Afterwards she gets to her apt. Goes inside and locks the door. She strips and takes a scalding hot shower and puts on her mini skirt and halter top and stiletto heels for work at the club and goes to the office after giving a nice hug to her cat Jake. She gets down there, says hello to Vie, and introduces herself to a couple of the other agents she has not met yet. She sits down in front of a PC and proceeds to fill out her report. She spends a good couple of hours sifting through her memory of dates and times and she also looks on her notepad where she has written down items for later reference.

After words she saves it, sends it to Alex, prints a hard copy, and files it away. Alex sees her report and says wow this is some report. I wish all my agents did such detailed work. I am very glad you are on our side. Linda smiles and says I deeply touched by that Alex. You have said nothing but kind words to me and you have been very open and honest with me.

Well you have better get to the club because my newest agent you will be making your first bust tonight. All you have to do is wait for Mike to show up, you call me. Me and all of my agents will come in and grab him and the girls you have pointed out. It will be a grand entrance for your first ever bust as a federal agent. But I will most likely be naked when you all get there. But that will not be the issue. I just want the agents coming in to be professional please. Oh they will be. I will brief them myself. I will send a text of the where and when I get it from Mike. All right then this evening is a go.

She gets to the club and is in the dressing room getting ready when one of Mike's girls comes in and says Mike needs to see you honey, something about a change in place and time. All right Colt I will. She finish's getting ready and walks to the bar and asks Mike, So what is the change she asks. Well I will go with you to the hotel. The client is a special one. We need to be careful with this one he pulls some major weight in this city in the crime family.

Ok I will treat him with respect and give him the best he has ever had. He will be bringing his wife with him as well. I can handle that as well. I am a Bisexual. I like both sexes. But I really want more than just a hundred dollars for this I want three hundred for both. Done and done Mike says you will not regret this. No Mike there will be no regret in this at all she replies! She goes back to the dressing room and sends a quick text message to Alex telling him the situation. The reply is we will tail you and wear the earrings and we will know when to come in.

After her second set that evening Mike takes all of her clothing again when she is fully naked on stage. She goes to the bar after her last set and says okay Mike what is the big deal. You see me up on stage butt naked why take my cloths again? He says because I can and two he hands her a slip of paper and it says it is time go get ready. He hands her costume back and she walks to the dressing room. She comes out a few minutes later in jeans, a very thin tight white cotton sleeveless T-shirt without a bra on. He said here is the address and I will follow you there. She gets in her truck and sees; Mike is following her! Farther back she sees Alex and some agents with him in his black SUV vehicle. She gets to the hotel room which is on the first floor and knocks on the door and a beautiful but older lady answers the door and inside is a man about six foot four inches tall and well built. Linda says Mike sent me. The older lady says please come in we were not expecting such a beautiful young woman this time. But Mike always seems to come through for us.

Linda says I do not know where Mike has gone to He was right behind me on the way here. Oh do not worry my dear. So Mike told us the asking price was three hundred dollars right. Yes that's right! Well that is not a whole lot so how does one thousand dollars sound. Well I like that a lot. But we have shall we say unusual tastes in what we like. What is that Linda asks? I am Bisexual if that is what you mean.

No dear that is not with that the man produces an asp whip and snaps it out. Oh shit! Linda says to herself. She says what in world do you want to do. My dear little girl the man says my wife gets off on my beating very beautiful young ladies till they are disfigured for life. Then I get to rape them. Linda gets a shiver down her spine at the word rape but quells the feeling. All right Linda says! She very quickly reaches in her back pocket and says all right let just stay calm and this will be painless. Painless she says the large man replies! What are you a Cop or something? Or something, I am a federal agent showing them her badge. Everything you have said has been recorded. She gets in to a classic sideways L stance and gets ready for him to come at her.

He says! Well anybody can buy a badge these days, I even have one but I took it from a dead cop a couple of years ago after I blew his brains out when I found out he was a cop. He steps closer and swings the asp. Linda easily circle parries the swing and punches him hard in his kidney. Then Linda lashes out with her left foot and catches the older lady in the solar plexus and she drops to the floor clutching her chest, trying to inhale precious oxygen.

Then the large man somehow gets his hands on her shirt and pulls really hard to get her off balance. But the thin T-shirt is shredded and Linda is standing there topless. The man makes the comment well you are a pretty one. I will enjoy taking you out. I do not think so and Linda savagely kicks at his family jewels and crushes his testicles. The large man spews forth a stream of bile, and vomit as the darkness takes him under. She then hears at the door a knock and she hears Mike. He says is everything all right in their she flings the door open and punches him with all her strength right in the solar plexus and he goes flying back into the parking lot and lands on the hood of his car. Just then two cars raced up, and Alex and several agents get out and rush to Linda's side.

Linda what happened? We only got the part that one guy was going to whip you. Well He tried to with an asp. But My Martial arts training paid for it-self. He takes off his jacket that says federal agent on the back and hands it to Linda saying we cannot have our agents going around topless in public now can we. Linda smiles and replies! I suppose not! She retrieves Mike and puts on two plastic handcuffs on his hands and ankles. After he has recovered a bit he says, so you're a fed huh! Yep and we have decided to help the locals with this bust. They are going to put you away for a long while. I will see to that and that piece of shit and his wife will be going to a maximum sentence for what they have done and the guy is most likely getting the chair. You could turn some evidence over and get your 30 years cut down to maybe to 20 years.

Then she says or I can let you rot in prison for all those years. But look on the bright side, three good meals a day plus a cellmate with the name of Bubba and he is looking for a new bitch. You look like the type that fits the bill.

Mike says! Oh no you don't you Fed's cannot do this. I know. Oh how do you know? Linda replies! Talk to us we can help! Okay He says I have to have some guarantees. Like what Linda says. The whole time she has been talking to Mike Alex and been right there with her. He is letting her take this one, okay I will see about you having a lighter security lock up and a reduced sentence. But it had better be good or I swear I will hand pick the big meanest smelliest guy in there and tell him you want to be his bitch. Alex cringes at that and sees that

Linda would try to follow through with her promise. Alex says I would listen to her Mike With her background she would do it. All right Mike says! So a few hours later Mike is taken away by the FBI and has been granted a speedy trial provided the information pans out.

That information is that those three gentlemen have been coming into the club for the past month. Always speaking in German, I know the language sense high school. She asks what have you heard or know about them. The one German guy always comes in and gets the imported beer that we have. He says that it is the close to his home's beer. If he is alone he will act like any other patron there gets up close to the stage and have chair dances, everything.

But when the other two come in they stay as far away from the stage as possible. Mike says I think their Iraq's or something like that. They're from over there. I get an instant dislike on my meter from them. With the whole 9/11 thing and all the terrorist threats we have had I just want to do my part? All right like I said if it pans out I will speak with the Justice dept. and see what we can do. Okay gentleman takes him away.

Alex says that was good, you're giving the next class on interrogation. But don't you think we had better get the locals in on the bust at the club for the girls. Yea we had better get there. I have had a Lt. Waiting for my word to go ahead. But you need to be there. All right see at the club, she sees the time and shit it is almost time for my next set. She hops in her truck and quickly gets a spare shirt on and gets to the club with five minutes to spare. She whispers to the owner who was wondering where she was. We got him. Now in about fifteen minutes just as my set is getting over with this place will be raided, be ready and only the girls I have identified will be taken away.

About then Linda spots Vie behind the bar pulling a beer and she taps the bar as walks by and winks at her. She gets to the dressing room and quickly changes into her costume. When she is on her fourth song! She was fully naked the local cops come in quietly and start to gather up all the girls.

One young cop stops at the stage and says you to miss I was ordered to get everybody. Linda says okay sir could you help me down. He gives her a hand and she walks with her costume to the front, there is Alex with a young policeman in a nice suit. His badge is out and he has a note pad that he is writing on. Alex looks up and says to the young policeman in uniform that has Linda gently by the elbow. You can release her! She is not a suspect she never was a prostitute for the bartender.

So that's where he is Linda exclaimed! The police Lt. said you can put your cloths back on young lady Oh sorry sir I am very comfortable without them on I just forget. Go get your costume on young lady or I will run you in just for the hell of it. Yes sir I apologize sir. Ah! I have had a bad day that's all. Again sir I am sorry! Alright then Toni Reynolds get dressed! Thank you sir!

She heads back to the bar putting her dress on and forgetting the silk panties she acts so flustered. She gets to where Vie is and sits down, says in a low voice. It seems the locals only know me as Toni. We are trying to keep it that way my dear. But you played it just right. So have a drink and right now. There are no patrons in the bar. You named ten girls and the owner is a bit upset that he has lost over three fourths of his dancers. But if they play their cards right will be moved to protective custody. The others will be taken away for a long time.

The next several nights Linda is asks to pull almost double duty at the club. She says okay we still need to get more intelligence on the German and the Iraq's. That means twelve whole sets but no chair dances until the owner can hire enough girls to fill in. The German guy does come in next week and Vie lets Linda know where he is. She sees that he is alone so she goes to his table after her set and she has come back out of the dressing room.

The owner has been able hire able five more girls so Linda is able to relax a little between set's. She asks the German guys if she can join him and he says yes Fraulin you may. Linda asks you are German. He replies yes I am but I have not been there for many years, I still speak with the language as my native tongue. Thank you it is fine! I know what you mean. As she sits down He says would you like one of those watered down drinks they serve here for you dancers. Sure she replies. He gets the waitress to bring him another beer, bring her a dancer special. She says I have not seen you in here before. Oh I have been in here a lot it is you are a new one here. I sometimes come in here with two other guys. But then we are to be left alone. Okay whatever you say. Well right now I want a full chair dance and I will pay double for you to get naked. All right at the start of the next set I will go the full five songs Naked for you.

That next day was her day off, she went into the office and filled out her report on what little she has found out, and then she started to work with the Langley and Interpol databases on these guys. She had on a wrap around skirt and her stiletto heels from work. She was really liking the way her calf muscles were looking sense she started to wear them. She walks into the front office and gets a mug of strong coffee and Alex calls her into his office and says have a seat Linda.

He asks Vie to come in and she shuts the door bringing Alex a mug of coffee and one for her. Alex begins with the job at the Club is done with We need to start to find where the Nerve gas is coming from and when. I want you Linda to head up that case. But Alex I am still just a green horn agent Linda replies. No you're not! You have proven yourself on many occasions and you will stop at all most nothing to get the job done. Except one and I can see that one. So as of now you have all the resources of the Justice Dept. to get that Nerve gas and all the agents here with the exception of me and Vie, are under you. I am your supervisor she is my wife and a damn fine agent. Alex gets a gold badge out of his desk and says with the power vested in me by the president of the United States of America. I present to you your gold shield.

Congratulations my dear Vie says giving a very big hug and Alex comes around his desk and shakes her hand and gives her kiss on the cheek and says I had a feeling you would work out here. Besides you are the prettiest agent here besides my wife. Well I had better get back to the computer search then. Oh what about Hans?

I will have to meet him a couple of more times. Oh do not worry about him he has left the country but Interpol has him in their sights. We need to keep track of him. I would like for them to send to us everything he does. I want what he does written down and e-mailed to us so I can see what he likes and study him. Maybe we can find a weakness a flaw we can use. All right I will inform them! But now Linda says I will, while that is taken place I am tracking down those two Middle Eastern types. The next several days' agents kept telling Linda what a fine job she did and that they were proud of the fact she got the gold shield. She went to Vie one night after everybody else had gone home and she asks why everybody so nice to me i.e. mean I do not mind it at all. But I wonder.

Well Linda Vie says all of us agents here have the gold shield. But you were the one to get it the fastest and that was the last one to be handed out by the Justice Dept. They did not want to give it to you. But several of our agents here heard about that and said they would turn their badges in if the Justice Dept. did that.

Oh my! I never wanted that. Oh never mind that now The Justice dept. finally let you have it when you did such a good job turning up that Terrorist plot that they changed their minds. Well I am beat so I am off to home and a quiet night with Jake. Why don't you come out this evening we are all off here, we will be at Shelton's just of off George street. About eight p.m. and wear something very sexy. I know you like the ladies and there are a few there. Okay I will Vie I will see you, Alex and the rest there. Yes you will. She goes home and gets changed into her running Lycra outfit, does a good warm up and runs it hard for four miles. Then she gets into her apt. Strips and heads to the showers and puts it on as scalding hot as possible.

Then she dries off and puts on some baby powder and a little make up and then puts on her very tiny black leather mini skirt and then put on the black leather vest that has black mesh on the back. Then she puts on her Black leather Stiletto knee high boots. She also has chosen to go with black silk panties too. She grabs her bag with her pistol and badge and hops in her truck and goes to Shelton's.

She has been to the place a couple of times to just see want is going on there but she has never picked up a companion for the night there. She parks about a half a block away but with her training and a pistol with her she walks with confidence. Nobody bothers her on the way there. She gets there and she sees the whole office is there and all the guys let out wolf whistles and yells hey babe where have you been. But she also sees in their eyes that there are just fooling with her. She sits down and a very familiar looking hand sets down an Ice cold draft beer in front of her. She turns and sees her best friend Jenny. She gets up and hugs her very tightly. She says I have missed you my friend. Jenny returns the hug and says I have missed you as well. She sits next to Linda and Linda asks her how did you know where I was?

Jenny says it was Alex or Vie who tracked me down and flew me from Germany to here. They told me that you were a Special Investigator for the Justice dept. now. So that is a big feather in your hat. Yes my friend it is. What of you? Does your friend know you're here? She and I parted company about a week ago on very friendly terms. So when I got the call to come see my old girl friend I could not pass up the chance and boy you sure look good. Well Vie Said to look good tonight because there might be some ladies here tonight. I had no idea.

Jenny says to Linda, Vie knows that I am a lesbian right. Yes and she knows about me as well. So it is settled you will stay with me. Linda had said that loud enough by accident that a couple of the guys over heard her and said Awe that's not fair we saw here first mocking the slurred speech of a drunk man. Jenny says Oh you think you saw her first huh! Well young man I knew her when she was just nineteen years old and she turned and planted a big kiss right on Linda's mouth. Then several more shucks and darns where said, Jenny let Linda catch her breath and they both sat down.

They ordered supper and more drinks came but sense Linda was driving she only had just the one beer. She knew she could eat then wait for three hours and not have any problems at all. Jenny on the other hand was drinking beer like it was water she was so used to the strong German brew that this had little effect on her. Other than going to the ladies room all the time!

Later on that evening Linda got Alex and Vie aside and said thank you for bringing her here. She is such a dear friend. I have missed her! Vie says I know dear!

I have Alex and everybody else here has their Family but she is all you have other than your foster mother. You will be getting one-week vacation in two weeks. Take it and go see your mother and spend time with her. Recharge your batteries. Then when you have come back Hans and his little terrorists will be looking behind their backs at us chasing them. You have done a great job of data base searches. We will be going around the world for a few weeks first stop will be Iraq. Second stop will be just you me, Vie to a special stop. You will there on your regular holiday at your favorite Nudist resort. But we will be working so no fun stuff. That I would not think of. But I do not think you two were the nudist type. Oh we are not. But you will teach us on how to act and some of the culture but at the office that means take tomorrow off young lady. Have fun with Jenny she is flying back out to her home in Germany tomorrow night late. Again thanks you two. She hugs them both and heads back to Jenny. Linda says come home dear we have some catching up to do. We do at that my dear. They get to Linda's apt. They go inside Jake is waiting on the end table next to the door as they come in. Linda then picks him up in her arms gives him a hug and a kiss and hands him over to Jenny who takes him and does the same.

She then heads to her bedroom and says to Jenny we can watch Casablanca tonight. I have it on DVD in High definition. Linda comes back out to her living room naked and sees Jenny has striped as well. They embrace each other and then go sit on the couch. Linda gets the movie going and they watch it all the way though. Jenny says I have not seen our favorite movie in a long time thank you! They both get in bed and fall asleep holding each other.

That next day was a blast for Linda and Jenny. They both eat and went site seeing and did a lot of silly girl things. When Jenny's flight was ready they kissed each other good bye in the airport and promised again to keep in touch.

That next day Linda went in the office and started to tweak the database search and sifting through mounds of information that has been sent to her. She spent the better part of ten days working on this.

Vie asked when she was going to go see her mother. Linda said I had planned on Monday. I was going drive their Sunday. It is a long drive from here in Indiana to Nevada. Then spend the week with her and then be back to work by that next Monday. Sounds good dear, keep in touch Alex always wants to know where his agents are at any one time. Once a day should be fine, all right Vie. Linda took Jake with her on her trip to see her mother. She did not want to leave him in boarding house for him. That was really expensive and her mother loved Jake as much as Linda did. So it was a winning situation for them.

She told her mother all about her new job. The unclassified parts and her first bust she had. Her mother said I am so proud of you my dear. But will this mean you will be away from home a lot. It could be Mom Linda replied. Well then it is settled I will move to a small town just a short ways from you as to not crowd you. That way I can look in on Jake and your place when you are gone. I suspect that Vie would be a good friend to make for somebody my age. You know mom you are right as always. Well most of the time all right Linda says!

Her mother calls a moving company and Linda says I will pay for this move mother and I will not take no for an answer. Besides I think you want to move as fast as possible. So let me see want I can do. She gets out her cell phone and speed dials Alex. She says morning sunshine I am checking in and I have a favor to ask. Could you get a moving company that can get my mother moved to a place local to me for my mother, Alex says I will let you know in about an hour.

Linda says okay mom Alex my boss says he will work out a lot of the details and you will be moved to a place near me by Monday. You will most likely coming back with be. That would be wonderful dear. That way I can see my beautiful daughter a lot more and there is a nudist resort north of us so we can go there when it gets warmer outside. That would be nice; I have not had any chance to go to one in the past few years.

One hour later Alex called and said we have a company coming today to look at what they have to move and will be there in the morning to start. I have already secured a place for your mother. It is a small two-bedroom house with a low rent. The landlords are old friends of mine and they know the lady moving in it an older lady, so they will keep the lawn cut, do the maintenance to the place. In fact I checked and your mother could afford this place all on her own. That would be great Alex I sure she will love it. Send me a picture of the house on my e-mail and I will show her. Sounds like a plan he replies.

Linda gets the pictures a little while later, her mother adores the house, and the rent is really great. Later that the day the mover representative showed up. He said we can get all this packed up inside of six hours and we could be at your new place by Tuesday if that is the address you are going to is in Indiana. Yes it is sir! All right we will be here at eight a.m. sharp, see you then. The movers showed up and everything went well all of Linda mother's things was packed up and ready to go in six hours. Linda double-checked the address they were going to and they took off. Then Linda went over to the land lords office where her mother had her apt and asked to see the manager. She was a nice young lady and said there is a penalty to get out of the contract early. What is it Linda asks!

She only had two months left on this lease anyways, so that's two months' rent right. Basically your right, so how much Linda asks? Call it seven hundred dollars and I will void the contract as of two days from now. Now that is wonderful Linda says Thank you! Oh your mother has been a joy to have here. She will be missed.

Linda pays for the rest of the lease and her mother signs it and they leave a forwarding address. Next they have all her things turned off and get set to stay a night in local motel that will take pets. The next day they start back to Indiana the next day and get they're a day and half later. Her mother will stay with Linda until the movers get everything all set at her new house. All the power is turned on as well as the heat and water. Linda says to her mother. You will need to get a cell phone instead of a regular phone they are just easier to use, I will put you on my plan, and you will not have to pay for anything.

All right dear if you say so. Linda went back to work that Monday feeling recharged and ready to take on the world she tells Alex. Well I am glad you feel that way because you just might be. All that work you did with the database and the information requests have paid off big time. We have full names and their where-bouts for most of the past three weeks. Hans The one German guy is German and the other two are from Iraq. They belong to the Taliban and they have been trying for some time to get nerve gas here in the States.

Also they have some heavy backing to pay for this. Our first stop is to Kuwait then on up to Iraq with a Special Forces unit to track down this one unit and see if we can get their information. This means we will be going on a trip and it is a good thing Linda you have your mother so close now. Linda looks at Alex and asked did you make the suggestion to her. No I did not Linda! Vie had no part in this as well. All right! Thank you for all your help the mover's are there now getting everything all set in place and I will be there in a bit to settle the bill.

Later that day Linda goes to her mother's new place and sees that her mother is all ready unpacking cloths, setting them where she wants them and Linda gets right in and helps her out.

When they are done they head out to eat at a local restaurant. Linda gets a steak, steamed corned, and a good salad, her mother gets the chef's salad. Linda tells her mother that this case she is on will be having her leave for long periods of time so Linda hands her a key to her place and tells her where Jake's food is and his Litter box.

That next day Linda is called by Alex and says we have a go in twelve hours get ready. All you will need will be here. By the way what size clothing do you wear? Linda gives her measurements and he says Vie will make sure your BDU's will fit right and other uniforms we will have.

Linda calls her mother, says well it is happening sooner than I had planned but it will work out. I need you to go to my Apt. tonight and then at least once a day after that and see to Jake, is that all right Mom? Sure is my daughter she replies! All right dear I will, but I will need a vehicle while you're away. No problem mom you can use my truck, the gas card will be in the glove box and the keys I will give to you in a little bit. She goes home and changed out of her dress and gets on her black jeans and steel toes boots and a long sleeve skin tight black shirt and then puts on a shoulder holster with her pistol in it and two spare magazines. Then a black jean jacket over that and dark glasses and her cell phone, charger with her badge in her back pocket and man's wallet with her I.D. a few credit cards and other things in there. Then a combat knife inside of her jacket as well. She calls the office and asks an agent to come pick her up and take her to the office.

She then heads over to her mother house and kind of shocks her mother a little when she sees her little girls all dressed up in black. Mother Linda says I am a special Investigator now for the Justice Dept. So sometimes I have to go into dangerous situations. Now I know you will worry. Vie said to call her anytime if you just want to talk while I am away. But please mother she is a busy woman running that office down there, Bake them some cookies or something like that. I know the agents down there would eat that right up like I use to. All right Linda I will. A little while later Linda hugged her mother, kissed her on the cheek good bye and hopped in the black SUV that came to get her and they went off.

Chapter Five

$\mathcal{L}$ater that evening Linda! Plus her team of agents all arrives at an air strip and board a C-130 Hercules Airplane. There are all dresses in black in one form or another. Linda changed into her BDU's at the office and she was briefed that they will all get weapons when they get there.

There first stop which will be Langley. They stop there, get off the blackened aircraft, and are escorted to a hanger where they get a hot meal. Then they go and select their weapons. Linda tells them we need to stick to only one type of ammo need as possible. So they all selected the M-16 battle rifle. With the M-203 Grenade launcher mounted underneath. Then they load up with five thousand rounds of ammo for the rifles with plenty of extra clips. Plus an assortment of grenades for the launchers and a couple of hundred rounds for there each of their personal weapons as well.

As well as level three-body armor and night vision gear and Kevlar Battle helmet. They board the plane again and settle in after it had been refueled and it takes off to Kuwait. Six hours later Linda gets everyone up and passes out maps and recent photo's of the two Iraq's we are after. But these guys have been known to reverse situations on most anything so we are going to have to be on our toes. Later on in the flight she is told they will be landing in one hour. She passes the message along and sends her own message to Alex giving him the update. After they land In Kuwait there are escorted to hotel down town Kuwait and Linda being the only female gets a room to herself.

But she makes do, keeps inside, and does not show her face anywhere. The next morning the team gets in a convoy going to Baghdad. From there they will make their way farther north to a smaller city where these terrorists are believed to be.

That night in the Baghdad hotel! While Linda was sleeping alone! Several individuals slipped into her room. One pressed a needle into her arm and then five of the men help hold her down with a very strong hand over her mouth. While she struggled until the drugs over took her and she went under into the blackness of a drug-induced sleep.

Several hours later Linda woke up hanging by her wrists. She was still naked and her legs were spread wide apart as well. She thought well here come the torture might as well find out what is up and work from there. I might die here to she says to herself.

Linda works her mouth and tastes the after taste of the sleep drugs. I hope the guys can find me she says to here self. A couple of minutes later a big man walks in and says in bad English. Woman why are you here with those American spies. Good he thinks I am not the team leader better let him think otherwise.

Linda replies! I do not know what you are talking about I demand to be released. I am an American here as an aid to the new base commander.

You mean to tell me you are a secretary I find that very unlikely.

Well it is the truth. He draws his hand back and swings with a full back handed slap on the side of Linda's face and she is seeing stars right now. She shakes her head slowly to clear it a little. He brings his hand back the other way and slaps the other side of her face and Linda tastes blood in her mouth and all she can do is hang her head and drool out spit and blood. Had enough you unholy bitch he says. Piss off Rag head she says sharply! He then punches her in her Stomach but she was ready for that one and she had tightened her stomach muscles. When he hit it felt like he was hitting an oak plank.

Linda just raised her head and said had enough asshole. Then he did quick one two hard slap on her face again and said I will have you broken very soon and then he said and I will enjoy myself with this as well as he puts his hand on her groin; very soon indeed. After he left another solider came in and slowly began to work on her. He would hit her numerous times in the belly and the ribs and other areas but he left the groin and the breasts alone and well as the mouth.

Mean while Alex had been informed that Linda had been taken and the only intelligence they had was a fuzzy video of them entering and leaving. All the Agents were looking everywhere for a clue to who had her. Agent Harris said to four of the men to go to the one site and see if you can get the info on those two Iraq's while we and many American soldiers start helping to find her. All the leads they have lead to a small cell of men who are still loyal to Hussein. They say we will check in every four hours, sooner if we have something Harris out.

Agent Harris tells the four agents best suited to go get the information up north. We will look for Linda here. I know you want to stay here but she would want the mission completed. Yes sir they replied. Now get your gear and go. Yes sir!

About a day later Linda is looking really bruised up good. She winces at the pain a little after the guy beating on her has left. She gently settles in to a comfortable position and lets her mind go to her work out routine. Her instructors at Commanders school told her and the class that the best way to survive was say nothing or almost nothing at all. But you need to have a mental escape. Think of the most fun thing you want to do, design it, and bring it forth. I encourage you to get creative. Build a car from the ground up or build a clock to the smallest and finest detail. But you must be able to do this at any time while you are captured.

They will know what you are doing but if your will is strong enough your sanity will prevail. Linda remembers the lessons well and precedes to prefect her work out routine down to the smallest detail. Several hours have passed and Linda has fallen in a state of semi sleep and they seem to be leaving her alone. They did soak her down with freezing cold water, turned the freezer unit on in the room, and turned it to ten degrees above zero.

He had come in and says to her. I will break you American spy. He lights a small candle and places it on a desk twenty feet away and says let us say we are not so cruel as to not let you have some warmth. He laughs loudly he walks out shutting and bolting the door after he is gone.

Agent Harris is at wits end He just called Alex again and still No Linda. Damn she could be anywhere. Just then a voice says on the radio on a secure channel. The marines picked up a young lady running away for somebody and through an interpreter she says they have an American woman tied up and naked held hostage.

They think she is a spy. Okay honey where is she being held. They get the directions and they all mount up. Agent Harris has her colt .45 with him. They soon arrive at the cluster of houses and with the Intel on this area of town Agent Harris has the team spread out and circle around the place. The marines hold back in case any take off. Capture them and then we interrogate.

They quickly move into the doorway's bust through smaller dwellings finding nothing or abandoned meals or very surprised families. Then Agent Harris sees a small crack in a wall and works his combat knife in it. The crack gets bigger and a rifle shot from the other side alert the others we have found something. Harris gets out his Glock 17. Shoots several blind rounds into the area and is surprised to hear a scream in pain. He grabs the door with both hands and hauls back and the door opens up. He sees an Iraq national guard in uniform trying to get to his AK-47. Harris aims and fires and hits him dead center of the chest. He falls to the floor dead as the hole exiting through his chest is the size of a very large softball.

He grabs the keys on the table and unlocks the door. He goes in and sees Linda. Shit she looks bad damn-it he says. It must be below freezing in here he exclaims! Then he hears from Linda who is there as she raises her head.

One eye is swollen shut and the other looks really bloodshot. She is one big massive bruise. Harris goes up and says well will have you out in a minute Agent King. Oh please! She says though swollen lips and puffed cheeks.

Call me Linda! Okay how do I look! Well can I have a date when we get back? That bad huh! Did you bring by piece Harris? Yes Linda I have it right here. Good I want that bastard who made these bruises and the one ordered them done. Linda stands up with a little help from Harris and says Could you get some water for me Just a little and not cold or heated I am just a little cold so let's get out of here! One of the Agents produces a canteen and hands it over once there back in the warm hallway. Agent Harris takes off his wind breaker jacket and hands it to Linda. She gingerly puts it on and it barely covers her up. She gets her colt .45, and jacks the slide back, and chambers a 230-grain soft nose hollow point bullet. She stands and finds she able to stand well enough and says let's move out and locate those bastards. Harris says we have team going north to scope out the situation up there. Excellent Harris Well Done!

They start to move from door to door and they only see empty rooms but with lots of computers and stuff. Linda says we need to seize all this and have it tagged for the boys at Langley to go over. Harris calls it in and he replies they think they have captured everybody that was in here. We need to get you a hospital to get looked at. Alex would have my hide and so will Vie if I do not get you to safety.

All right but you are in charge while I am gone and let's get out of here. Outside she sees who they have in custody. When they get out there she sees they have both men that had done all the damage. She tells the SGT holding them that these two are special and need to be interrogated by the Folks from Langley. She gets on secure radio and calls the specialists in on these two to find out any and all information and why she was targeted. Then she is transported to the Military Hospital there, she is seen by several doctors. Some minor surgery for the eye! Medication and lots of bed rest.

The next day Alex shows up and she sits up in bed and says hello sunshine what brings you here to this part of the world. As if I did not know! Well my newest agent your abduction and torture. Have they found out who those guys were yet?

They told us everything once we used the sodium pentothal on them. The one kid who was beating on you is a known woman hater. So his motive was clear and he will get a long sentence. The other we are still working on him. The only thing we have so far is he had orders to grab you from a higher up. You will be glad to know Alex that Harris did a fantastic job here. Finding me and getting the mission completed.

Yes your right he did but he did what he was trained to do. Some of his emotions got in the way. Please do not be hard on him. I will not be! I am fond of you as well as everybody in the office that's sweet Linda says! Let's get me out here for some rest and recuperation time my mother will want to be told to. I will figure what to say to her. But I can sift through that data we found at the site and see what that holds for us.

The next day Linda is up and around there tent they have working on her report but taking it easy as much as possible. Alex and the team came in, saying that lead up north was almost a dud. If Harris here had not sent that team up there we would have lost everything. Good job Harris Linda says. It is confirmed they will be getting a tanker of VX Nerve gas sometime in the next three months from an old East German operative.

I believe we know who that is. Linda says Hans. Yes you got the prize. His full name is Hans Greuber. He has contacts in the former Soviet republic and with a lot of the old army stockpiles at his disposal. Let me set up a database on his personality and work from that. Okay let's get cracking on that and take it easy today. You promised the doctors to do that. I am, I am sitting down and only doing just what I need to do.

Typing does not hurt. It is when one of the guys here cracks a joke that's when it hurts to laugh. All right finish your report and set up the database and get some bed rest, I have a nice soft cot brought in here for you so use it. Yes Sir Linda replies!

She finishes her reports and sends copies to Alex and the base Commander, plus Military Intelligence and the CIA. Afterword's she goes and lies down on the cot and sleeps for a couple of hours. When she wakes up she finds Alex and the base Commander there quietly talking.

Then she recognizes the Commander when he turns around She says well Sir how have you been? The Commander replies! Agent King now is it. The last time we talked you was a Major under my command. Now you are a special investigator for the justice Dept. that is a big leap. Congratulations are in order. Why thank you sir as Linda stands slowly and Alex went to her side to help her up. Alex! Linda says I can walk you know. Yes but the doctor's say. Oh piss on them sometimes. I know my own body, better than they do.

She walks over, gets a cup of hot water and a tea bag, and sits down with them both. Well Col. Belkens it is nice to see you again. How are the wife and kids? Oh their good? Helen still wonders if you will ever marry. Well now that I am no longer in the service of the Military, you can tell your wife that I will never marry a man and it is a fair bet that I will never even date a guy at all.

So you are telling me in a roundabout way that you prefer females to us guys. I never said it. But yes I am one of those. But please do not get me wrong Colonel you are a great guy to be around and a good friend. I did have several men as friends with who are still good friends. Alex and a couple of the agents here are like that now. He turns to Alex and asks is everything she telling the truth. It is Colonel and she is one of the best agents I have and the very the privilege to work with other than my wife.

All right Linda he says. I see your reports are as good as ever. You are still the best looking female officer than any of the other female officers I have ever worked with I can say that now. That Colonel Belkens I will take as a complement. You are very welcome. Now if you will excuse me I have a base to run. If you could in the next couple of days hobble over to the command tent for the next staff briefing and surprise Charlie Howard. He is charge of the Security Police here and could use a pointer or two.

With that he leaves and Alex says that went well sense you just about came out and said you were a Lesbian. They might be able to come back and say I lied in the OSI investigations. But the questions were too general and I was able to work around them and tell them the truth and still deny everything. Now as to the database search on Hans I need more. I am narrowing it down but there are some missing pieces. Like what does he like to do where he likes to go on vacation? Stuff like that. I will get it.

The next day Linda feels a lot better and she decides to go and walk a couple of miles on the track the base has laid out. After that she stretches with the bases health director and therapist.

She feels good afterword's and walks to the showers and gets a hot shower and changes into clean black BDU's pants and a T-shirt and she pins her badge on it puts on some wide sunglasses and goes to the base staff meeting with Alex. Afterword's she gets to see here old second in command and tells him a dirty joke. He laughs like he always did at one and then says it is good to see you again. I was sorry to see you retire like that.

But I see the Govt. still hands their hands on you again. Yes Charlie they do but I call a lot of the shots. But my Supervisor is a good man. One of the best I have had the privilege to work with. Now how are your reports going? I know you hate to do them so do I but they have to be accurate. That is why they always liked mine.

Afterword's back at their tent the whole team is there and they are filling out there reports and Linda has set up a laptop to see what information has been sent in. and she sees an opportunity. One piece of information on Hans is he is a womanizer. Loves to look at and/or paw females and have sex with them as often as possible. One place he loves to go to is a hedonistic style resort in Jamaica. Linda sees this, calls

Alex over, and says I think we have a place where we can get him. He goes to a place that I like to go to on vacation. All though for different reasons! But Linda that is a nudist resort you cannot walk around with your badge and a gun. Besides did you not say something about this earlier to me? Yes I did come to think of it. That has never stopped me before. I was stripping and I could not have those items up on stage with me. You are right. But this time we take our time. When we get back to the office we need to get a team ready for that as well and I know you will not want to have a male companion. So you will not.

This is the place you have been going to for all these years now huh. Yes Alex it is and I am known down there as an Air Force Lt.Col, I could have gotten a promotion by now. That could be a reason I am down there. All though he would recognize me from the club! He has seen me naked on a couple of different times.

Alex steps back and looks at Linda and wonders why she is not hurt more from all the torture she went through. All the below freezing temperatures the base doctors wonder why she does not have frostbite on her toes and fingers. Now here she is going over a plan to help find out more from Hans. He says sit down Linda I need to ask you a few things all right. Okay Alex She sits down.

Alex asks why are not suffering from frostbite? I just got the medical report from the doctor, it said; you only have a mild case of exposure! Alex! I learned a long time ago in Command school I learned about how they use captive and torture techniques.

There were mental techniques that involved having a good frame of mind and the understanding that you very well may die. I put myself in that frame of mind and then I went to a place in my mind that they could not touch.

Granted only somebody who has been studying the martial arts for many years can attempt to do that. I had my Sensei teach me this. She knew my love of working out so she said keep designing your workout routine the whole time change it around. So that's how you beat the system. To a point all that water they sprayed on me, and the threat of the one guy coming back to rape me. I was terrified! I was in no position to resist in anyway.

I am over that now I will do my job for you without reservation and by any means necessary. I believe you Linda but you do not have to sacrifice your morale beliefs for this. Linda replies. I have thought about it and that is one of the things Jenny and I talked about. She has taken a male as a lover and she says she was well rewarded. If it works out that I have to take Hans to bed I will need counseling after the mission. All right Linda I will see to that.

But you just get well and heal up you and two other agents will be going with you to this place. Which two Alex she asks. Vie and I that's who. Oh that's right you said something about you going. No but we have always wanted to go but this will work out well. Vie will be there for you if need be until a better person can help you if the need comes up and we all could use some sunshine.

The doctors finally release her for full duty and it is time to go back home. She comes home and Jake leaps right into her arms, pushes his head under her chin, and is purring really loud. Her mother comes up to her side and wraps her arms around Linda and Linda returns a one armed hug. She says hi Mom how have you been? Oh good. That Vie has been such a sweet dear I would try to call her only every other day but she would call and tell me what she could. She said you were hurt over there but you were fine and looked at by the best military doctors. I am fine now Mother nothing was broken and all but a few places still has some swelling. But I can work out like I want is the best news for me. Sometime in the next month I will be going again but on a working vacation with Alex and Vie. We are going to my Favorite Nudist resort. Oh I know the one. I suppose I cannot go with you. No mother you cannot go there with me. Like I said it is a working one. But you can help. Get with Vie in the next several days and tell her about all about the customs and nudist life style. She is a good lady she will need to know. She can then tell Alex I will help them too.

The next few weeks goes by quick enough and Linda in now fully recovered. There are no more bruises and no swelling anywhere.

She is back to running five miles a day and an hour and half weight training. She used some heavy weights to get good results fast. Then a scalding hot shower a little alone time with Jake and a bowl of hot buttered popcorn. She would also go to the practice range and get really good with her colt 45.

She also works up a dossier on Hans and possible hiding places. The Justice Dept. is ready to seize his entire holding's he has here in the States. Everything is ready and Linda feels more energized each day. Her workouts have been getting her into even better shape and she has even more muscular definition. She has even studied for and got her third degree black belt in her martial arts. She tells Alex I am ready, as I will ever be. I have been seeing the Counselor when time permits and I can do what it takes. He says that is good because you might have to. If he finds you attractive enough but I will also have an operative on loan to use from the CIA she has never said anything about sex being an issue. So it will be who can get the information and none the less said the better.

I am with you on this but the Dept heads wanted somebody just in case you got cold feet. That I understand Alex I do not like it but I understand. I understand all too well Linda. I was once forced to have sex with another woman, and I was only married to Vie a little less than a year. I was also horrified that she was ordered to be on the stake out team as well. But I preformed my duty and retrieved the information and I spent the next year feeling lower than whale shit. But Vie stuck by me the whole time. The Counselor you have now! Was the one to help me get over what I felt like she is good! Alex I feel I could go to bed with a man now but only if he was a special man. If I had to go to bed with Hans I would get sick afterwords away from him. So as to not get the mission in trouble, that comes first. All right then Vie has been getting lessons on the lifestyle from your mother and you have given me a few pointers. I really appreciate them. It will be hard to keep from getting excited at first. Just look at them as if they all had two hundred extra pounds on them. Well that might work except when we see you. Just think of me in this business suit. I will do my best.

Okay I am going home to get ready. I need to pack a lot of sunscreen and some clothing. Not much but a little and my favorite towels. She gets home, and her mother comes over, they have a good supper, and she says this working vacation will most likely be two weeks long. They stay up a while talking and watching an old movie called Father Goose. It was always one of the funniest movies she has ever seen.

That next day she drives over to her mother's, leaves the truck there and gets picked up by Harris in a black SUV. He says I wish I would go with you to that place you get better looking each day. Well tiger just cool your libido this place is not about sex. It is about the culture, the sun, and not much else. Sounds boring! It can be if you make it that way. I spend my time just swimming in the ocean and getting a deep dark tan without tan lines.

They get to the office, Alex is with Vie, and Harris drops off Linda with her one bag. Alex says Doris will be here in a minute she just called. Sure enough another black SUV pulls to a stop in front of them and a young looking lady wearing tight jean shorts and sandals with a string bikini top and a large handbag says hi everybody my name is Doris.

Both Alex and Vie were dressed for the weather. It was 50 degrees and raining outside and even the outgoing Linda had on black tights and a black fleece pull over shirt with a black crop top underneath that and a light trench coat with her running shoes. Doris says what's with all the clothing people you're just going to take it off anyways. Linda says your right but I was cold, I am sure Alex and Vie were cold as well.

You younger aged people can do that. We cannot. All right then let's get inside and get ready. Doris leans over to Linda and says so are you the other bait for this Hans guy? Linda says! Yes I am I will do what I have to do. I do not like it but In the interest of national security whatever needs to be done will be done. Doris looks at her and says boy you are really brainwashed. I do it for the fun of it. I just like men! That's it and this stuff for my country is good and all but don't you think you're taking it a bit too much acting like that. Damn you must act like you were in the military before becoming an agent.

Linda's look in her eyes sends a message that she was. Linda knows the young agent is dedicated so she lets the comments slide away. Doris could you come on over here Alex says we need to get your ticket and then you two can formulate a plan once were there. You two will have separate rooms. Our room will be in-between them so if you need help we can get there as fast as possible.

Boy sense when did you become the scout leader Doris says? I am the team leader and I have the rank in the Justice dept that says I can young lady. I will also point out that my wife and Linda also have the gold shield in the Justice Dept. So when we get there you will be whom your passport says, Linda will be an Air Force Colonel I had you promoted from Lt.Col. I was right you were ex-Military As Doris confirms her suspicions. Yes I am a retired Lt.Col with twenty years of active honorable service. Okay Linda I do like you a lot. You have spunk let's see if we can get this guy and find out what we need to know.

They left for the airport and they make sure that they will have access to their hand weapons when they get there. They have a whole Lear jet to themselves and Alex proves to be a good pilot. They have a light lunch of Cold cuts and vegetables and fruit. Doris eats some but says I need to keep this figure looking good.

Then she looks at Linda who has taken off her coat and fleece pull over off. She also has about four times the amount of food on her plate; then Doris does. She sees Linda's stomach muscles and says where do you work out Linda? Those are the best six-pack abs' I have ever seen, and how do you stay in such excellent shape with all that food. Doris these have taken about twenty years to perfect them and it takes even harder work to keep them and to fuel them. But if you want when we come back I will instruct you on how I achieved this body. You have a deal Linda Doris replies!

The next few hours goes by quickly. Linda says we have to stay clothed until the hotel limousine service picks us up. Then inside there we can disrobe. They land and Alex makes sure the Jet is serviced and parked ready for them to take off when they decide to leave. Linda has her trench coat in her bag now as it is 83 degree outside and sunny, Doris says this will be a good assignment she can feel it. Alex leans over and says every time she says that the assignment she was on go bad somehow. Not bad but it does not work out right. I will keep a look out Alex.

The limousine pulls up and it has a real heavy tint to the whole back section. Vie gets in then Doris and then Linda and then Alex, Linda says! Hello Man how are you today. Good and you Mame! She gets in and the door shuts behinds her and she says if you want you can get out your clothing now. Linda pulls off her Crop top and they see she is not wearing a bra. Doris is getting naked as well. Then Vie says Might as well Alex. They all start to disrobe except for Alex. Soon Alex is feeling the urge looking at three naked ladies one his wife of thirty years whom he loves dearly and two other beautiful ladies that could grace the pages of a well-known men's magazine. Linda says remember what I taught you Alex. I will try Linda.

They get there, they step out of the limousine, and the Driver says welcome back Lt.Col. Linda says sorry Raul I was promoted I am a Full Colonel now. Thanks! It is wonderful to be back.

He helps everybody with his or her bags. Alex decides to keep his shorts on and flip-flops. They get to the check-in counter and Raul hands Linda's bag to her and says it is good to see you again I hope you stay is a wonderful one. Thanks Raul!

Doris is seeing a lot of everything and says to Linda how can you stand it? With all these gorgeous guys all naked here. It is easy Doris I for one do not see them that way and two I am a lesbian. Doris looks at Linda again and says to her, with that smoking hot body you have honey you could have any man you want.

Let's get to our rooms. She helps Alex and Vie with their bags and says come on you two lovebirds. She says loud enough. That was the cover story that Linda is bringing her boss with his Wife on a second honeymoon and she is bringing a family friend along as well. They get to the main suite for Alex and Vie and they all go in. Alex says to all three ladies could you please cover up and let this old man relax some. Vie puts her robe on. But Linda says Alex you need to calm down my covering up will not help. Vie be with him. She moves over to him, and sits down next to him. Now take some deep breaths. Doris is sitting very quietly. Soon he feels at ease and opens his eyes while looking at Vie. He says if I picture you in your suit at work it works a little. But how do I keep this guy pointing to his little head from attracting attention. That Alex I do not know. Vie maybe you can help him with that. Vie says you know I think your right. Linda stands and grabs her bag and says come on Doris I want to see if Hans is here yet. Let us see how sharp your talons are my dear young lady.

They leave Alex and Vie to spend the afternoon taking care of his problem. Mean while Linda has unpacked and got her sunscreen on and went to the beach. She sees Linda basically trolling around looking for a Hans looking type guy. Linda had checked the hotels list of guests and his alias name was not on there. So let her have fun Linda wanted to soak up some sun and run on the beach later. She ran for five miles on the sand and then when into the ocean to cool down and rinse some of the sweat from her.

She walked out of the ocean and towards Alex and Vie Both were naked now and Alex's little problem seems to be gone and Vie has a nice smile on her face so did Alex. Linda gives her a hug and says you are glowing my friend and so are you Alex. I am concentrating on trying to keep myself civil. Well let me go get a shower, the salt-water plays hell on my hair unless I get it cleaned out fast. Doris should be meeting us in a private dining area for supper. I am starving, so are we Vie says Okay in fifteen minutes says Linda and Doris does know where and when. Linda heads to the outdoor showers and turns them to scalding hot and gets all cleaned up, she washes her hair and lathers her whole body. She knows the effect she is having on every guy who can see her. That is her intention to cause this.

After her shower she will dry off and apply baby powder, comb out her hair and wrap it in a towel. She takes a fresh clean towel from the ones ready to use and goes to meet Alex and Vie. They get to the Semi-private dining room and Doris is they're looking all nice and tanned.

Linda says their seafood is about the freshest you can get. Linda gets a large Lobster with sirloin steak on the side and a salad with iced tea. Alex gets Crab cakes and macaroni salad. Vie get a shrimp dish with a salad. Doris on the other hand gets a small steak with sautéed button mushrooms in a butter sauce and rice. She says I have an allergy to shell fish and I did not see baked fish on the menu. That is fine Doris. But they do I know I get that a lot when I am down here. You seem to know this place well. How long have you been coming here?

I have been coming here about ten years now so I should know some of the customs!

Oh and by the way I think Hans will be in tomorrow. So have your fun tonight, because young lady, you get first crack at him. He knows me and I will stay away from him. He knows me as a stripper at a bar in Indiana. But if you cannot get the info I will troll for him and see what I can do and any information you can give me on his habits in bed will help. But you said you are a lesbian Linda.

Yes I am! But I will do want is needed to get the mission completed. I will do what I can says Doris Most men are putty in my hands when I have plied them well. But I will help you tonight okay! So later that night after the dinner Alex and Vie go off and see a movie together. Linda and Doris go to Linda's room and Doris shows Linda what she should expect from a guy, Linda repays Doris with a lesson in female love. They wake the next morning early and Doris goes back to her room and gets cleaned up. Linda goes to the beach for a morning swim and uses the outdoor showers again. She then meets everybody in the dining room for an Ala Carte breakfast. Linda orders a four-egg omelet with three different cheeses inside with wheat toast and orange juice and a large bowl of fresh fruit. Alex has a waffle with bacon and lots of syrup and hot black coffee. Vie gets a plate full of fruits and some vegetables. Doris gets a bowl of fiber cereal with skim mike.

Doris still marvels at how much Linda eats. She asks how you stay in such great shape Linda. I run about five miles a day some times more when I am at home and I lift weights for over an hour each day. But at my age I warm-up for at least a half an hour before running or lifting and the weights are at a medium heavy level. I do not do light weights any more.

By the way my resting heart rate is forty-two beats a minute. I am a third degree black belt In Tae Qwon Do I also eat six to eight thousand calories a day mostly protein and some carbs for that needed fuel. Did I cover about everything Doris? I would say so, except you are as uncovered as we all are! Linda, Alex, and Vie all laughed at the joke and Linda says to herself. This young lady has what it takes to be a good officer. Just a bit more seasoning with the right people and she would be a good agent.

After breakfast Linda says lets head to the beach for some sunning I want to darken my tan a bit and Doris you could to.

We are supposed to be here as friends. Alex says Vie and I are off to a honey honeymooner's afternoon set up by the staff here. So you two keep your eyes open! For you know who when he shows up.

We will Alex! Vie take good care of him as she whispers in her ear. I liked that glow you too had yesterday.

Linda and Doris spend the morning on the beach just walking around and Doris is openly looking at all the men while Linda is looking at the ladies. Then a big limousine shows up and as soon as it pulls up Linda says that may to be him. I cannot be seen!

With that she quickly says you know what to do. I will be close by in case he gets difficult. Sure enough when Linda is far enough away, Hans steps out of the Limousine fully naked and female greeter hugs him and says welcome Herr Hamlin to our wondrous place. We are over joyed that you have returned again.

Thanks! He replies in English but heavily accented German. He goes inside and Doris follows them inside but from a distance. She decides that a slight seductive pose would get his attention. But she does it in such a way that it was not aimed at him but to look very natural for her to do that. He does spot her and makes a note to see this young Fraulin later. He goes up to his penthouse suite and then goes to the singles bar where anything can happen. Doris sees him head in there.

She heads out to the beach and waits for Linda to talk to her. She says! At least he is somewhat good looking. So I will have an easier time with him myself. Yes Linda I have taken men to bed for our country that were very fat and smelly.

Those were some disgusting times. But with a little help from an excellent counselor I am still able to go through with these assignments. So I do know a little of where you would be coming from! If you wind up in bed with him! Thank you Doris! You are becoming a true sister to me. Okay go get him and follow the game plan and here are those earrings we told you about. They will be different that the ones I had in Indiana. These have a half a mile range. But I will try to get closer than that if everything goes south. Remember little sister stay frosty when the heat rises. Later that night when Linda hands the hearing device over to Alex so she can get something to eat. With all the trash that Hans is saying to Doris and to several other young ladies in the singles bar. Linda would really hate to go in there to troll for him. Later Alex hands the device back to Linda and says listen carefully Doris is going to bed with him tonight. Let us hope she will get some info out of him. Linda resigns to the fact that there will be the sounds of lovemaking in her ears so she just listens for words spoken and if something goes wrong.

The next morning Doris gently knocks on Linda's door and Linda opens it up. She let's Doris in and says do you have any coffee I need something and a shower. I feel a little disgusting. Linda says please help you're self, then sees her hands shake a little. Hey their little sister what's wrong.

Are you all right!

That man is a pure terrorist I feel so dirty now.

Her knees get a little weak but Linda grabs her, supporting her, and gets her to the shower. She turns it on not scalding hot but that hot for Doris. She carries her in the shower and holds her there for a while under the hot water. Soon Doris feels a little better.

But lets us get out of the shower now. I will take care of you. We need to get you a little help. They get out of the shower and Linda dries her off and leads her into her hotel room and has her lay down on the other bed in there. She turns down the bed covers and gets her under a sheet and places an extra pillow under her head and kisses her forehead and says I will have some hot green tea sent up and I am calling Vie she can help you better than I can.

Oh please do not leave me Linda. He was so horrible; I cannot describe what he was talking about. She decides that Alex needs to be here as well. Soon Vie is over talking quietly to Doris. Linda and Alex are listening to the tapes of last night and Alex finally finds an answer.

He has a radio jammer in his room and from what I can tell she was drugged. It is a drug used by soviet agents to scare the shit out of those around them. The drug has powerful mind altering effects. Some of the after effects are extreme terror and extreme nausea it was most likely put in one of her drinks. I will have Vie draw some blood and I will send it off. I have a small test kit here but it is very limited.

A few hours later Alex says there was something in her system, So Linda I am afraid it is up to you. Well there is one thing in my favor. We know who and what he is. What he can do to that he dominates that night.

Oh boy I will be going to bed with a man. Alex! Linda says now I need a hug! It is okay dear as Vie comes from behind. Vie has taken to the nudist lifestyle readily and Alex is getting use to it. So both were naked as they both gave Linda a hug and said I still have those earrings you used in the club job. Those are a lot harder to jam and you can watch your drinking.

So that afternoon Linda took in some sun and a six-mile run, did her usual shower as close to the singles bar as possible. As hoped here came Hans out wondering around. He had his towel and he then spots Linda. He smiles and comes over. He says Toni is that you in his German accent. Han's is that you? She asks. It certainly is! What are you doing here in Jamaica? Soaking up these wonderful rays my club hopping man! I make enough each year in tips to come down here for a week or so and just lie on the beach and get no tan lines.

But Call me Linda down here everybody thinks I am an officer in the Air Force. Hans looks at her and says you are a stripper and not in the air force. But when I first started to come down here many years ago I found out they do not like my kind of person here. So I made up a story and have stuck to it. Ah! I see Linda. How's about a drink in this bar they have good drinks in their not those watered down ones you have to drink. All right lets go then.

They go inside and the atmosphere in this singles bar is like no other. Linda hardly went in here but a few times and always left alone. The people in here usually had sex openly. She was not really into that. But now she had to play up a single woman looking for sex.

Throughout the early evening and the night Hans was buying her drinks and she was doing her best to sip them and tries to get rid of it if it was drugged. He was also touching her and openly groping. Linda felt really disgusted and finally says Hans I cannot wait, let's go back to your room, and make love all night. What the hurry sugar they are having a dancing contest and I want you to enter. I have seen you dance you could beat these people with ease. Oh okay Hans!

Soon the dance contest starts and she goes into her routine of dancing around the stage to get tips and all the guys in there are screaming for more when she is up there. Well I hope Alex is getting an ear full on the receiver for these earrings. I am feeling really disgusted and sick right now that this guy just wants to drink and screw.

After the dance contest which she wins hands down. Hans says! Let's go back to my room for some loving. They get back to his room and soon they are making love and all Linda remembers is to go to her place in her mind to get away from the really disgusting parts of this sex as possible. His breath is raw from all the beer he was drinking and he is not a gentle lover. He is very rough with her and after he is done he rolls over and goes right to sleep. Linda says to herself do not cry now. Remember the mission. Look for evidence get copies of everything. She slips from bed. And goes to the bathroom and wipes herself off and promises herself a very long scalding hot shower.

Then a minute later she quietly opens the door and gets the syringe filled with the sodium pentothal Alex had left there just a minute ago. She goes over to Hans and injects the drug in his butt, waits for a few minutes. Then she starts to look for his laptop and other things. After about twenty minutes she finds his laptop and cell phone and the jammer. She brings all three to Alex and Vies room and hands them over to him.

Alex has a grim face on and Vie gives Linda a hug and holds on. Vie says my young sweet agent I know the pain you went through. Come here and let me help you. Alex leaves them alone while he works on copying every scrap of data on his devices. Linda's shoulders are shaking with a good cry and Doris is awake, and gives her a hug. She says my true sister you are very brave. That is a horrible man.

That drug he gave me made me terrified of him. I am very glad you did not get it. Both Linda and Doris embraced each other, coming away sniffling and wiping tears from their faces. Linda says I feel better now. But I need to get back there quickly and finish the night with him. Alex says I am just about done. You have done an outstanding job and you as well Doris. The drug he gave you has no known defense other than time for it to get out of your system.

Thank you Alex She replies! Linda gets up, goes to the shower, saying! I need a shower before I go back there. Vie says help yourself dear. Vie whispers to Doris follow her in a help her scrub her back and be gentle with her a shower is only what she needs. Doris follows Linda in and sees that Linda has the water on full scalding hot, just about as scalding as you can get it. Doris says that will not help. I have noticed that all your showers are as hot as you can make them. You were hurt once a while back?

How did you know? Did they tell you?

No Linda I know the signs I was raped once myself so turn the water temperature down some and I will come in the shower with you as a sister. I do not want sex and I know you do not want it. Doris steps in the still really hot shower and helps Linda with scrubbing her back and helping her. Linda cry's a couple of minutes and she feels better. After they come out they dry off, and Linda gets Hans equipment and goes back to his room. She enters slowly and quietly she quickly replaces everything where it was, and she makes triple sure the radio jammer that Hans has.

That is appears to be working correctly. Then she crawls into bed with him and orders herself to sleep a light sleep. She wakes several times the rest of the night when he moves around. That morning He gets up and he has what most guys call morning wood. He looks at Linda and says how's about one for the road Okay.

She steels her mind she says okay Hans! Sounds great to me they have sex again she not only hates it more but when she gets back to her room she is retching so bad Alex came in with Vie right behind him with pistols out. He sees she is in the bathroom still getting sick. In between her getting sick she says Alex what was I supposed to do say no! He would have thought something was up. That's it we have the information we came for. He has about ruined two of my best operatives on this type of undercover work. We are leaving within the next four hours. Vie help her here I will get a doctor to look at her in the mean time and Doris to.

Four hours later Alex was right they were in the air, both Linda and Doris were sound asleep. Alex is just getting off the secure radio and having Hans followed again. Also the doctors found some of the same drug in Linda's system as well. Damn it that man has to be stopped. Linda wakes up enough to hear this sleepily says he will be Alex I will die getting him and she falls back asleep.

Vie looks at her husband of thirty years and says that is the toughest female agent I have ever known, even tougher than I am when I was younger. Then they hear the sounds of a deep snore from Linda and they both smile. After they land Vie calls her mother and has her come pick her up. She will need some time with you as a mother. Plus she will be seeing a specialist for what she had to endure for this mission. Please do not ask her about it. It is still classified. But if she says anything to you please remember only speak to us about it and nobody else. All right Vie I will. She is to have the next two weeks off to recover and thank you for your advice Alex and I had a wonderful time despite the mission.

Chapter Six

The next week was pure hell on Linda. She finally told her mother what happened, at least the non-classified stuff. They both cried a lot and held on to each other. She talked to Jenny, told her the same thing as her mother, said I do not think I could ever again be with a man. Jenny replies and says my dearest friend I am so sorry. I wish I could be there to help you. I have my mother here to help me, a very good therapist as well.

They talked for a while more and Jenny felt her friends spirits lift up a bit. She said Linda remember my friend I am just a phone call away. I will try to get some time in the next couple of months to come see you. I would love that Jenny, Thanks good bye my love Linda says! Bye my love Jenny replies!

Linda had got up the nerve to get on her regular work out clothing a week after they got back and had a very satisfying five-mile run. Then she went back to the weight lifting and with in the week was back to her normal workout routine.

After the two weeks was up Linda come into the office and Alex said Come in please. You are sorely missed around here. Thank you Alex I need to come back and continue my work. I want to take Hans down really bad. We do to and welcome back. The report from the therapist said you are ready and I will never ask you to do that ever again. I understand how you feel. Thank you Alex! That means a lot coming from you. That also is from Vie as well. But let's get back to business shall we.

I have a little bit of good news. I have applied for and received permission to have a CIA operative assigned with us permanently. You don't mean Doris. Yes I do. You yourself same she had great potential in your report and that carries weight with me. So as of tomorrow she is assigned to this office. She will be assigned to your team but like all the other agents here I am her supervisor.

Has she been getting help like me? Yes but her help was to one getting rid of the drug that was still lingering in her system. Also when that was finally purged, she remembered several more details of Hans. Also the same drug was in your system as well. But your body reacted differently to it. After we ran further tests we found a reason and a defense of sorts. Your body had a lot of lactic acid in it. From my five mile run earlier that day and the dancing contest in the bar Linda says. It is a start on a cure for it.

So that dossier just got bigger by a lot. I am working on getting a gold shield for her to. But do not tell anybody that until it goes through. You got it Alex. I need to trace Han's movements and those other two guys. That may take a while.

The next day Doris shows up and Linda greets her with an open smile and a warm hug. Doris wipes a tear from her eye and says Hello my sister how have you been I am very happy to see you well. Well let's show you around and set up your cube. All right Linda Alex says but I need you and Doris in here for a briefing in fifteen minutes and bring some coffee or tea when you do.

Wow! You get to bring coffee to a briefing. We are a family here. Vie is our mother so to speak. She will help you with just about anything. By the way do you have a place to stay yet here in town no! I was going to look this weekend. Well you can stay with me Linda says and with a little peck on the cheek and in my bed if you wish. Doris hugs her, whispers in her ear I would love that. Let's get you settled.

They move her box of desk knick-knacks inside and get it settled and hand's her, a spare coffee mug. Linda has hot green tea in hers and Doris asks can I have some of that. Sure thing, they get to Alex's office and settles in. Agent Harris is there as well. Alex says Linda you will be the lead on this small side case. All the work has been done. In fact because of you this case came about. You remember a certain Frank that kept you from advancing in your job. Yes Alex I do. He could not see beyond my tits for one and he was a foul-mouthed chain cigarette smoking SOB. Well here is something you caused. They started to look at what was going on in that factory and certain items came up missing. That factory produces timing valves and delivery systems for chemicals.

All highly commercial grade as good as military grade and your old supervisor's assets have grown in the past three months. We have traced the money through over twenty different holding companies and as many fronts. But the money comes from the same bank accounts as our friend Hans. Linda's jaw hits the ground as Alex reads the report. Damn Linda exclaims I would have never thought that SOB would stoop that low. I knew he has very bad judgment in not liking our govt. and being very open about it.

Well Linda you and Doris are to go to your old security company's office and bring another Security officer with you to take over for Frank as he is to be relives of his job and placed under arrest for his acts against the United States.

Linda I know you will enjoy this. Your Right Alex I will. Besides he hates ladies in authority over him. As the briefing gets over with Linda says he may retaliate. Do what you need, but get all the information we can get. Doris still has the backing of the CIA so if that is needed do what you must. Can do Alex she replies.

They head out to her old security company and they go inside. The receptionist recognizes Linda and says welcome back Linda it is so good to see you. Did that Private Investigator job work out for you?

Hi Kelly how are you! Fine she replies!

Linda takes out her badge and so does Doris and says Kelly I am not a Private investigator. I am a Federal Agent for the Justice Dept. and this is Agent Doris Trine. We are here to talk with and pick up your Human resources manager and a security officer and take them to the plant where I use to work. Kelly asks do you have any weapons on you. Of course we do Kelly it is the law that all federal agents be fully armed at all times. Please wait right there I will send them out. They're waiting for you.

Linda is starting to get a little pissed off right about now. Doris senses this and says hey take it easy she is only dong her job. Yea I know but as federal agents we have to be armed at all times. Let them play there little games. We have the law on our side!

A minute later a security officer comes out and he is armed as well and one of the company's VP's comes out to. Linda recognizes him as the one who helped with her two-week notice. Hello Mr. Morris I am glad to see you again. Hello Agent King! It has been a little while sense you worked for us. Yes and you know why I have came back.

Let's get there before that bastard gets away. Oh do not worry about that Linda. The other officer there is my man he is keeping an eye on Frank at this very moment.

They all leave and Doris drives the black Govt. SUV to the plant that Linda used to work at. They park at a side lot and the Human Resources manager there greets them at the side entrance and sees Linda and asks are you the one coming back to work here. I really wished you could have stayed you were the best security officer we had here.

Thanks Stacy but no! They go in through the factory and when there at a certain spot Linda motions for Doris to be ready we need him alive if possible. Also you to the new security officer with them do not draw your weapon unless fired upon we have the authority here in this so pleased back us up just in case.

He says with pleasure Agent King.

Linda and Doris both come from within the factory and quickly approach the guardroom. Frank sees Linda and says well if it isn't big tits herself. Shut up Frank that will be enough.

She sees that he now has a pistol strapped to his side and asks well Frank sense when does carrying a piece to work part of the job. That happened about a week after you left us here. Something about terrorism, Linda reaches in her blazer pocket and pulls out her badge.

Frank just looks at it and laughs. Sense when they give badges to a little bitch like you? Oh Frank I think you are missing the big picture here. This badge is real and this man here; she gestures for the new security officer to come forward is your replacement. You are under arrest for the crime of conspiring with terrorists to kill thousands of innocent's lives.

She hands the warrant over to him and he hands it back a minute later. Linda has not even put her hand on her pistol but she knows Doris is ready. Well Frank what will it be? Hand over your weapon and you will be escorted to a maximum-security cell to await your arraignment. Linda does not even get the next words out when all hell broke loose.

Frank pulls his own pistol and starts to point it at Linda. Linda's leg lashes out and snap kicks upwards as he fires the pistol. Doris has her pistol out, takes aim, and shoots his hand with the pistol in it.

Frank starts to run for it and cradling his bloody hand. Linda does a low sweeping kick and trips him. He falls to the floor and Linda lands on his back with a pair of plastic cuffs and quickly cuffs him. Then she asks the other guard there who she did know and says hello Tom and would you please get me a first aid kit and call an ambulance. Doris gives him the number, Thanks!

Oh Doris that was a damn good shot where did you learn to shot like that. My daddy taught me how to shoot.

A little while later Linda calls Alex and says Doris had to shoot his hand but he will regain full use of it with time and therapy. We will be back inside of the hour to fill out the reports and such. Linda you did a good job and tell Doris the same thing. Oh I will. She closes the phone and says Hey Doris Alex says excellent job and I am saying the same. That was some excellent shooting. Well Stacey I hope this has cleared up several things for you. Now that this happened we can keep a better eye on the situation here.

She looks at the one VP that has been there the whole time and says you need to screen all employees of your whole security company through homeland security. This is as of now a national security matter. I will get that cleared but you need to start the process and Stacy you need to work on getting the security equipment here upgraded. I will see about getting you access to a low cost loan to help.

Thanks Linda they all said about at once. We appreciate the help and the forewarning. That usually does not happen with a warning like you just gave us. Well I have had the time to do some reading on the regulations and we can help.

They finally get back to the office and Linda puts the requests in, marks them urgent, and puts her signature to it. She then fills out her report and helps Doris with hers then saves them and prints them and sends everything to Alex he comes in and says Doris I see Linda has helped you with your report. Yes she did Alex!

That is fine her reports are some of the best I have ever seen and I have seen your old reports you needed a little help their young lady! Yea I guess I did.

Do not worry Doris Linda says I have helped everybody here. It was one of the things that helped me when I was a Commander in the Air Force.

But it is time to go home and sense you are bunking with me let's go. I need to work out when I get home and you need to meet Jake. Who Is Jake Doris asks?

Alex says you will find out. Doris asks do I want to know. Yes you would but I want it to be a surprise.

They get to her two bedrooms apt. and when she comes in Jake leaps up into her arms and begins to purr real loud and rubbing his face in Linda's. Linda turns to Doris and says Doris Meet Jake My cat. Linda hands him over to Doris who takes him and smiles real wide. How did you know I loved cats! Well your old supervisor let us know. Doris says! Well I never could get one by Carl!

Linda closes the door and says I am going to get changed to work out do you want to come along. Sure but I do not have my work out cloths with me. Linda replies if you do not mind you can borrow some of mine. There real clean, sure Linda comes out of the bedroom wearing her running shoes and nothing else. Doris says Is there a nude running place here and Linda says I wish but here which ones do you want the hot pink or the royal blue.

I will take the blue ones, and Linda sets them on the kitchen counter and gets into the pink set, they were very short tight Lycra shorts and Lycra Sports crop top. Doris sets Jake down and sets her bag down. Then takes off her clothing and steps into the same type work out clothing that Linda has. Not much in the way of covering and thin, Doris asks don't the cop get called sometimes with you wearing these work out cloths. I mean there practically see through. Not really! Then again we are federal officers now so what could they do. Besides I run mainly away from public eyes.

I now go armed with my badge, I have, and extra waist pouch that will hold your pistol and badge and some water. That would be great. Then they go outside and Doris remembers it is still cold outside and says why don't we go and run on a treadmill it is freezing out here and we do not have much on. Your right Doris but you wanted to know how I work out and getting this smoking hot Body as you called it. This is what I do. Besides you will warm up soon enough!

Linda says we warm up first and sense I am forty years old now I need to take my time, and stretch and warm up right. So for the next half an hour both Linda and Doris help each other warm up. Then Linda asks how far you can run Doris. She replies about three miles at the most. Okay then a three-mile run.

They start out slow and when Linda sees that Doris can keep up she opens up it faster and Doris calls out I cannot go faster. Linda slows down, and jogs beside her and says you can today Doris I know it. Now push it I will be right here with you.

Right at the three-mile mark Doris seems to hit the wall and can barely walk. But Linda says you need to walk it off Doris. That way you will not get cramps and you will cool down better. I will be back in a few minutes I need to run three more miles and I will walk with you. Then Linda takes off like a jackrabbit and about sprints the last three miles. She slows down next to Doris who is still breathing heavy, as is Linda and they walk together in silence for a few minutes. Then Linda has caught her breath she says to get better at this you need to always push your self-harder.

During my short capture by the Taliban in IRAQ I used my mental discipline to help me get through that ordeal. It also helped when I had to go to bed with that pig of a man Hans. Doris says I am sorry about that Linda I could not help myself. Now do not worry Doris. I read the toxicology on that drug he used and it was some nasty shit. So do not worry. What is done is done! I am dealing with it.

Like tonight you will be with me at my place because although my foster mother is a great lady I need a female to hold on to tonight. Just hold onto! I'm not looking for a female companion, which I know you do not mind. Doris says I was hoping to spend some alone time with you anyways, you have been like a sister to me.

When they were cooled down they headed over to her apt weight room and went in. She put on a six-inch wide weight belt, gave a three-inch wide one to Doris, and said this is my old one. Sense you will be only lifting light weights that are all you will need. But I will be doing the heavy weights. Just enough for definition! To keep your muscles long and very lean.

After about an hour of weights Doris is ready to drop. Linda says you did well today. Inside of six months you with have an excellent start on a body like mine. You said just a start! Man that is a killer she exclaims. Well I did tell you on the plane going down to the assignment that it took me years to get like this. Yes Linda I remember. Linda replies saying you have good genetics it would most likely not that you nearly as long. They get back to Linda's apt and go in.

Linda goes to the shower and strips out of her work out cloths. She calls back to Doris and says we could save water and shower together I would love that, Doris comes back and strips out of her work out clothing and Linda puts her arms around a very tired and sore Doris and kisses her. Doris returns the kiss. Linda then starts the shower and sets the temp to not scalding hot. She tells Doris I still love the temp scalding hot. I have grown use to it over the years. But for you my dear I can turn it down.

They step in together, lather each other, and then clean each other's backs and Doris helps Linda with her long hair. They get out and dry off and Linda walks to the kitchen still naked, and says I am fixing my high protein meal for supper and I am fixing enough for a couple of meals you are more than welcome to share with me. I am the host and you are my guest. The only price is a kiss for the cook. Doris says that is a price I will pay gladly.

About an hour later the last of Linda's plate is cleaned off after she has had two big servings of her very high protein meatloaf with Broccoli and fresh roma tomato's and fresh brewed green tea. Doris had a full slice of the meatloaf and said it was very good, very much like her mothers. It was getting about 8 p.m. that night and Linda said I would like to watch a movie you can watch with me if you would like, I have My Darling Clementine.

Who was in that oh it is the original Ok corral movie? Yes it is Replies Linda! Sure that sounds fun. But can I ask you a question. Yea sure! Doris are you always like this so nice to people. I try to be! I guess you could say that. That was something else, you seem to always go naked when you are in your apt yes I am and when I am at my Mother's house. We are both nudists. My mother has asks her landlords if she can buy the place and they said they would think about it. Of course I would be over there a lot helping her get it set up so she can have a fenced in back yard.

They both sit down on the couch close to each other and with a large bowl of popcorn and watch the old time movie. Doris says this is wonderful. I have never had such a nice evening. Why thank you Linda cleans up the kitchen a little and asks you can do one of two things sleep with me in my bed or on the couch. Doris says putting her arms around Linda saying I want to be with you and passionately kisses her. I cannot this early after what Han's has done but you are welcome to hold me and I hold you tonight. Doris says I would love that my sister.

The next morning Linda is up early as usual and Doris is having a hard time moving she is so sore from her work out. Linda says you need another very hot shower. So Linda helps her up, walks her to the hot shower, and gets in with her. Then Linda turns the heat up a bit and Doris wants out but Linda says this will loosen those muscles up. A few minutes later Doris's muscles do relax! With Linda giving her muscles a gentle massage.

After the shower Doris says I feel better, still sore but better. Linda says get dressed we have to be in the office by seven a.m. and we need to leave by six a.m.

Doris looks at the clock and says it is only five in the morning! She exclaims! I have not been up this early in years. Well get used to it under my roof Linda says! With a sly smile or I will you wake up. I am retired military and we always had to get up early. I use to get up at four thirty every morning to workout. Doris says! I might like that kind of a wakeup call. I bet you would and I know I do. My roommate in the air force when I first went in, we had become lovers. She woke me up a few times like that. It was great but all good things must come to an end.

Linda says get dressed, we need to get going. Doris asks sense this is Friday can we can wear casual clothing to the office. Linda comes back and she has on a pair of Black Lycra Spandex and a black spandex sleeveless top.

Oh! What are we doing an op today? Oh yes and jeans would be just fine. Linda says is that Bengay I smell?

Doris says yes and could you get it on my back pleased. Then they have a quick breakfast of eggs and Linda says I do not bacon here I never eat it all though I love it. They have some fruit and eat several eggs scrambled with cheese and orange juice, Linda says we will stop and get coffee at this little place I know it has the best coffee.

Sure thing my friend it is six a.m. when they walk out the door. Linda is wearing her black spandex outfit, and long black trench coat. Doris is in her old jeans, field jacket with a long sleeve flannel shirt underneath. Both had their weapons in combat shoulder holsters with extra clips.

They get to the office after they stop and get coffee. Vie says hello you two you're here before anybody else besides Alex and myself. Linda says that means I am on time.

Doris sits down in a chair and massages her leg muscles and says what kind of an op are we doing today Vie! Well Alex wants to do the briefing. My legs are killing me. What's the matter Doris Linda run you to hard last night Vie says, well? Yes But I also did it to myself. I want a killer body like she has at forty. I am only twenty-four years old and even though I am considered very good looking by a lot of people. I prefer a fit harder looking body like Linda has. That is not a bad goal.

Soon the rest of the agent's file in and they all head to the coffee room, and get coffee or tea and go to the main briefing room. Alex comes in and following behind him is a local police Lt. the one that was at the strip club with the clipboard and threatened Linda he would throw her in jail to.

Of course he did not know she was a Federal agent at the time. She says morning Lt. how is it everything going? He looks and does a double take. He says but I saw you in that strip club and you were naked.

Yes Lt. I was naked, I was also undercover as it were. As it were indeed.

Alex says well sense the niceties have been exchanged let's get this show going. In steps a state police Capt. and two Lt's. Alex says we will be assisting the state and local police today with a situation that has escalated almost out of their jurisdiction.

It seems our two gentlemen that we are looking for have had a drug operation going on here for some time. Sense it does involve these two terrorists I have asks the locals that we at least assist the arresting policeman and we all sign as the assisting arresting agents. We will fill out our reports accordingly. The State police are here for the same reasons.

All right agents and officers we roll in fifteen minutes. Agents take SMG's and handgun and make sure you wear your vests. I also want to have you each team up with one other person who will watch your back. Linda sense Doris is not familiar with this type of op take her with you. The rest of you pair up and remember people stay frosty when we get there. These are gang style hoods that would love to take down a fed or a cop. So follow your training and we should have very few problems.

They all get in Black SUV's and head to a place on the East Side where there are abandoned houses, The pull up two blocks away and the only thing they see are about eight fully tricked out cars sitting in front of the one address. There are several guys outside smoking and opening carrying weapons. Alex says this is going to be trouble. They will see us coming a mile off. Linda says roll right up into the yard. We have our badges out and ready. We all know what to say. That could work Alex replies!

The quickly plan for all of the vehicles approach very quickly and converge around the house and if there is resistant just follow procedure. It appears that all the locals have left the area for the time being.

The first part of the plan works generally well they have to return fire after they get out and tell them there under arrest. Linda yells Justice Department Federal agent Hands up Now! Of course the gang member fires at Linda but Doris shoots him in the knee and yells at the kid! You want to lose the other knee? I would suggest you drop everything and stay still we have an ambulance standing by.

The outsides gang members quickly give up or die shooting at the deadly marksman of Alex's team. Then the Police Lt. says you guys work quickly. I like that. Alex says thanks but we need inside and quickly. Alex Says! Linda in his throat mike! Take out the front door, and stay frosty. You got it Alex 30 below zero! Linda and Doris go to the front door and they get real low to the ground and place a small charge on the door. Linda points a small radio detonator at it and pushes the button. About one ounce of C-4 plastic explosive blows the door off the hinges and Linda and Doris roll in and come up on the feet ready to drop anything that fires at them. There is nobody here but there is a small red light flashing in the next room. They do a bounding over watch approach to the room and when they get a look inside.

There is nobody inside but there is a medium sized cylinder case that has been slide open upwards. Inside is a small round bar about 3 inches longs and 2 inches around. There is also something next to it as they both get near it; it is a Geiger counter that is going clear into the danger zone on radiation. Linda sees this, grabs Doris, holds on tight, and pulls her with her out of the house at a full run yelling in her throat mike that they need a HAZMAT team in here now. There is a highly radioactive isotope in there and both of us have been severely exposed.

Linda says get everybody out of there. Doris come with me they get to the next house and find a hose still hooked up and says this will hurt but it will help believe me. Linda says strip off your clothing as Linda starts to do the same. Alex sprays them down with the water and have the ambulance take us to the near hospital that can treat radiation exposure.

After they leave Alex orders the HAZMAT team to search the house and they find twenty dead gang members from radiation. Alex also gets a report from the HAZMAT team that the stuff inside was very nasty. Even a short exposure can be very serious.

They inform the hospital what kind of radioactive lethality it was. The HAZMAT team checks over the rest of the agents and the police they clear them and Alex heads to the office, and gets Vie and says let go to the hospital. I want to check on my two Agents. They get to the Hospital and find Linda in sitting in a bed with one of those Hospital gowns.

The doctors say! I can go home here as some as the paperwork in done. But Doris will have to stay a few extra days. Even though I was a lot closer to the isotope my much denser muscle saved me. Doris on the other hand got about a hundred and thirty milli-rads. My work out last night hurt her a little bit.

I have talked to her and she does not blame me but I blame myself. Vie says oh come on Linda she wanted to work out with you to so come on let's get you home. All right they said the trick of spraying us down washed a lot of the radiation away. By the way Alex I suppose this is another lead for me to try and track down. Yes Linda it is. But we will get you home tonight and tomorrow we add this piece to the puzzle. We should have more information of the isotope in the morning. Linda signs the release paperwork and they wheel her out of the hospital, she is still only wearing the hospital gown. Vie says are you cold Linda. She replies! No not really not when just a few hours ago I was standing outside naked and Alex was spraying both Doris and me with a hose. I was cold then. Vie looks at Alex and he says She said to do it Vie it was a fast way to get the radiation washed off of them. I could tell you were staying frosty then Linda Alex says. Linda replies you could say that. Vie glares at Alex and does not say anything.

They get Linda home and she goes in, and takes a long hot shower and fixes some of her leftover meatloaf and curls up on the couch for the rest of the day. That evening Doris calls and says I will get out of here in two days so keep my side of the bed warm for me. Linda replies! Of course I will. You just rest. I am not even allowed to work out tonight so it is a movie night then work in the morning. I will stop by tomorrow after work and see you okay. All right lover, see you then. After her movie she takes her medication for the radiation she has absorbed, and strips and goes to bed. She is up in the morning at five a.m. She dresses warmly and goes for a brisk walk after three miles she gets home and takes another shower and takes her medication again.

She get dressed for work, she selects a her black suede knee high stiletto boots with a knee length black suede skirt and a white silk long sleeve blouse which she leaves the top few buttons undone. Under that she puts in her back-up nine millimeter pistol to belt holster with extra clips in a few pockets. She puts on her black suede leather jacket and her Badge inside a jacket pocket and goes to work. Once there she heads in, and tells Alex good morning sunshine and says thanks for picking me up at the hospital and taking my truck home last night.

Well it was better than having another of the agent go out of their way to do it. Sense I live the closest and I have somebody that could pick me up. It was a no brainier.

Linda heads to her desk, and fills out her reports and files them and sends them to Alex. She also does what she can for Doris's reports. Then she calls the nuclear regulatory commission and sends them the information on what they have on the radioactive isotope. She wants to know where it came from. Also she checks the local hospitals and clinics for any unusual illness that could be radiation sickness. She marks this national security level and has Alex give his signature for it.

About noon when Linda is eating a very lean chicken breast and a salad at her desk, information starts to come in on the isotope. It was a mix of Strontium 90 with Plutonium, and some u235 thrown in to make it even nastier. Also information comes back that for the past six months there has been strange illness in that area. But the gang that was there told officials that they were paid to be there and sell crack cocaine. Which they were doing, but there was nothing in the house to make it. They were able to get an address and made a huge drug bust at the real place where they made the drugs. Only the gang leaders that stayed away from the house and only had minor illnesses could give us a description of the same two men we have been tracking. So that is something else we need to look out for.

Linda goes to Alex and asks to come in. He says sure, How you feeling by the way. I feel fine. Just wish I could go work out. But I did a three-mile walk this morning. That's good Alex says! So what did you need?

I think we need to get the international community involved with this. They have upped the ante and we need to respond. I agree with that, so where do you want to start at Linda? I was thinking we start to get by bringing in a few of those known Al-Qaida cells we know about and let the CIA or the NSA work on them for a while. To me they're suspected terrorists. Anything we do to get the information within reason is fine by me.

Later that day the Nuclear Regulatory Commission get back with the office and says we may have found out were that chunk of rod came from. It is Russian and it came from the Chernobyl reactor. Linda replies to the man she is speaking with and asks but that place was shut down and encased in concrete years ago. Yes it was but this was some of the stuff that was pulled out just before it was entombed.

This is some of the nastiest stuff ever produced. It's great for a reactor, makes power rather well but a bitch to get rid of. You have been a big help sir, if you would please file a full report to the Justice Dept. and Homeland security on your findings that would be great. Your welcome Agent King anytime we can help just call.

She gets her report ready for Alex to look over so he can add it to his. They are about ready to go Global on this and Alex wants all of his ducks in a row as the saying goes.

After he sends it off He says go home and get some rest you have earned it. It will take the high ups a few days to give the answer. I just hope they agree with us. Me to! Because the first stop will be London England at Scotland Yard.

Linda says I have a gut feeling that they have something happening there as well and they do not know it. I will send some inquires first, but we should be with them. I will also send what we have to Interpol and tell them what's up.

One more thing we need to warn the joint chiefs that something might be up and the national threat rating could go up one notch. But the new anchors should only know that it is just a routine escalation following the United Autoworkers Union Strike on present working conditions. Is that all Linda Alex asks? I think that covers it other than the President being told. I will take care of that Alec says! And everything else, now go home and rest. Yes sir! Linda replies! She gets ready to leave and calls her mother and she says I called Vie and we are having dinner tonight over here.

I would say so sense I am supposed to be there to help mom. Yes dear you are helping me cook. Too bad Doris cannot come she is still in the hospital. I will be over after I take care of Jake and go see Doris. She gets home, spends a few minutes with Jake, and tells him I have to go see Doris. She then makes sure he has plenty of water and food. She heads over to the hospital and goes to see Doris and she is sitting up in bed with an IV sticking in her arm. Doris says the food here sucks. I want some of your Meatloaf. Oh Doris Guess what! She brings out a throw away container full of her meatloaf and a plastic fork and knife. That should help a little.

Linda kissed her friend and said until they release you take care! Then you are under my care. I will follow the doctor's advice on how much you can work out. All right Linda take care love. She leaves and heads over to her Mothers place. Once there she hugs her Mother. She goes to the kitchen and helps her Mother make supper.

They prepare her Mothers favorite Macaroni and Cheese. Linda chops up the salad and puts in shredded carrots and cheese and homemade croutons. She gets a couple of small bowls and puts chopped hard-boiled eggs, and onion slices, and sunflower seeds, and olives. Then she pulls the roast out of the oven and covers it with foil to let it rest. Her Mother sets the table and she puts a pot of hot water on to make tea. Her Mother says I asked Vie to just come in and yell out when they get here.

About fifteen-minutes later right when Vie said they would be there, they both hear the front door creak open and Vie call out! Hey ladies you all home? Yea come on in were both in the living room. Vie comes first, then Alex comes in saying it is freezing outside and he looks up and sees Linda there as well as her mother and says Linda how's dinner coming along and can I help? Oh no just sit down, dinner is about ready

Later Vie explained that after the mission in that Nudist resort in Jamaica. I was missing that feeling of freedom without clothing. Linda's Mother helped me understand what I was feeling. So I had her set up this dinner with Linda so we could get together and they would explain more of the life style of the Nudist. Alex looks at his wife and at Linda, then to her mother, Alex says well I must confess that once I got calmed down I felt great. The dinner will be ready in a few minutes.

They then get seated; Linda says I will serve dinner! She brought out the salad bar and the steamed sweet corn then she brings out the Roast and carves up thick slices for everyone.

Linda asks which one they want, and she has them hold their plate up and it gets piled on as well as the Mac and cheese and the corn. Dinner went well. Afterword's they all went to the living room and had hot tea or coffee. Linda's Mother explained about the Nudist or naturist way of life. Some say Nude some say Naked. Well to me Linda's Mother said they both say the same thing. If you are interested in this life style on a vacation basis then try a resort like you all went to. Linda and I have been going they're for a number of years or there is a place in the northern part of Indiana that is nice I hear.

Alex says! Well we will have some thinking to do on this. Linda and her Mother give them a hug and say that it was nice to have us here and it was a great evening. The meal was excellent to.

They left and Linda helps her mother clean up and goes and kisses her mother good night and says Doris will be out in a day or two could you make some of your Chocolate chip cookies for her. She would love them. I promise not to eat any of them. Oh Linda you know all you have to do is ask and they're yours. I know mom.

Linda leaves and gets home and Jake leaps into her arms. Then she sees why. Her apt has been ransacked and her laptop gone. She closes the door, pulls her weapon, and checks the apt out. It is empty but the place is trashed. She gets her cell phone, and calls Alex and says send a federal forensics team to my place now. My place has been ransacked and my laptop is gone. Good thing their only going to find is nothing. He says we will have somebody over there as soon as possible. You know what to do. Yea! Touch nothing and try to piece together what's left afterwards.

The forensics team comes in, Linda is forced to sit through them going through her things, and they are not gentle. But soon they are gone and they say you should go to another place for a few nights. We have some prints and a couple of things that they were not careful about. Linda calls her Mother up and asks can I stay there a couple of nights, I was robbed, and the apt has been trashed. I need to bring Jake as well. Sure can my daughter come on over. Linda brings Jake over with his food and spare litter box. She sets it up in the spare bedroom and gets ready for bed. Then she comes out of the bedroom naked as usual and goes to the kitchen with her medication. She takes her radiation medication and sets down the glass.

She hears a noise from her mother's room and a muffled yell. She sprints to her Mother room to see three large men their wrestling with her 70-year-old mother.

She has stayed in decent shape for many years. Linda launch's at the first man with a flying sidekick and crashes into his chest. He falls to the floor. She spins and does a reverse crescent kick on the second man and catch's him across the jaw. She hears a loud crunch and he crumples to the floor. Then she hears a loud snap and an even louder scream of pain from her mother as the third man has brought his elbow on the back side of her mother's left elbow and the joint snaps.

Linda sees red and a fury rages in her she leaps across the distance and snap kicks the man in the face twice back and forth. Then she lands and a rigid knife hand jabs him in the kidney and he collapses to his right knee gasping in pain. Then she grabs his hair, and pulls his head back and curls her hand into a tight fist and just as she is about to bring it down and crush this man's throat. Her Mother tells her with pain in her voice. Linda please I will live don't kill him.

She just does a hard slam to his solar plexus and he goes down for the count. The first man is trying to stand and Linda says! To him you want to have a broken arm as well she grabs it and twisted it hard. He again gasps in pain, as the shoulder becomes dislocated. He says I will be peaceful. She lets him go and he falls to the floor cradling his arm, he says how in the world could a naked bitch like you take on us three?

Easy Linda says she is my Mother and you picked the wrong lady and the wrong place to do whatever you were going to do. Linda then strips the men of their weapons and pants. She ties up their hands with the pants, and calls Alex again for the second time tonight and says we have a leak. Somebody knows about me, my work. They just tried to get my Mother and if I was not trained, as I was in Martial arts they probability would have me as well.

Granted I will send a team to deal with those guys and you get your mother to a hospital. Alex we need to send some of our people over to the hospital for Doris. Alex says I will ask the CIA to do it. She is still CIA and they take care of they're own. She helps her Mom get dressed in a thick robe. Then some people get there in a few minutes to pick these guys up. She retrieves some spare plastic cuffs and is none to gentle with the guy that broke her Mother elbow. He says you can't do that.

Linda says I could care less what happens to you. She is my mother; you do not mess with MY MOTHER she exclaims!

Bitch he says! Linda says I can be, and gets up and walks to her room for a minute and gets her black jeans on, and boots and black sweatshirt. She hands they're weapons over for the team that comes and gets them.

The three men complained that Linda was cruel to them but they tell the assailants to shut up. Linda gives a short report of what happened. The Agents say I wish I could have been here to see it. A naked female agent taking on three full grown men that are fully armed and she takes them out, but before she can one of them has to break the elbow of the naked agents mother. Linda shakes her head at the comment! Men she mutters!

Linda says could you hurry up a bit I have to get my mother to the hospital, and I want to check on our other agents.

Yes Mame they say we will be in touch tomorrow about this. They tell Linda's mother they are sorry for the length of time it has taken. Oh think nothing of it! Take some cookies with you before you leave. Linda will show up where there are.

They leave with two dozen cookies and Linda locks the house and takes her Mother to the Hospital. She does not have a coat on just the sweatshirt with her combat shoulder holster on with a colt .45 automatic in it. She has three extra long clips with her and her badge is pinned on her sweatshirt. She helps her mother into the hospital and gets her looked at. She says while a Doctor is looking at her and getting her arm set that she is going to go look in on Doris and make sure there is somebody there to protect her.

She gets to her room and sure enough there are two very ominous looking men with the dark glasses and radio earpieces in one ear. They see her badge and let her pass. She says thanks gentleman and goes in. One follows her in and her evaluation steps up by one. She sees Doris, and she is awake and Linda says you know this guy jerking her thumb back at him.

Oh yea that's Scott he is kind of protective of me. Sense we are kind of an item in the agency. Item Linda says! Yes Linda I wanted to tell you but you have been so nice to me and everything sense the agency has kind of split us up by sending me here. But Doris the way you acted down there at the hotel in Jamaica you wanted all the guys there? Oh do not get me wrong! I did but I really have eyes for Scott. Scott says I really appreciate what you have done for Doris. You have saved her life and her sanity. Well she has saved mine as well. I will ask Alex to see if we can pull a few strings and get you assigned to our agency here. I am not saying I can do anything but I will ask. That is all I have hoped for.

Linda says good bye to Doris, and says to Scott, you are a very lucky man. She goes down to the emergency ward to see her Mother and her arm is set but she needs to stay the night. Mom do not worry I will have the police here and I will be here to.

The police arrive and she gives them instructions to look in every little bit and see if everything is all right. I will be here to.

I will be staying inside with you mother. All right dear but you get some sleep, that radiation poisoning still needs to be taken care of. You're right as usual mother.

The Doctor comes in and says time for sleep Mrs. King. You too! He says to Linda, you need to go home. She points to her badge and says I am staying she is the victim of a terrorist attack and I am a federal officer. She is under my protection. All right then just do not disturb her. I will be quiet sir Linda replies! She is my mother. Oh he says I did not know! Don't be. I am just glad she has a good doctor. He leaves and the cop sets up just outside the room and Linda helps her mother get comfortable in bed. Then she turns the lights down low, gets her coffee, and nurses it. The cop changes shifts and Linda asks the one cop leaving to bring her some fresh coffee and hands him a five dollar bill and says keep the change but make it a very large coffee.

He comes back fifteen minutes later with two very large cups of coffee and hands them over to Linda. She says thank you and he says I know what it is like. I hope you get the bastards who did this Oh rest assured I all ready have. I caught them in the act. I dislocated one guys shoulder, and shattered the jaw of another, and all three are having a hard time getting over I was able take them out while I was naked. You were naked the cop asks. Yes I was about ready to get in bed.

I was taking my medication and I heard a muffled yell and I went running back there. Those guys never saw me until I was pounding on them. Good night agent King I hope those guys get what they deserve and more, me to. Get some rest. The rest of the night Linda does get about four hours of sleep and she leaves her mother at five thirty a.m. She gets breakfast of just six hardboiled eggs in the hospital cafeteria and milk. Then she gets to the office and files her reports. She also sends the request to Alex that Doris's boyfriend Scott to be transferred her to his agency. It could be better all around for the whole place to have them together.

She hears the front door open and she goes up front to see who it is and Alex comes in with Vie and both says they are sorry that her mother was hurt so bad. I was just glad I was there to stop them. Alex says we have a briefing in one half-hour. This is a big one! So bring a lot of coffee it will be needed. I will get it made.

I have already filed all of my reports this morning. Alex asks when did you get in? About six fifteen a.m. this morning! I spent the night in my mother's Hospital room. I got about four hours of sleep and I have taken my medication. Alex says then get into the black BDU's you have here and steel toe boots. Okay after I get the coffee going. Linda gets all the coffee pots brewing strong coffee and gets changed into her Black BDU's she straps on her own pistol again after it had been decontaminated of radiation. She heads in to the Briefing room and gets her notepad ready and sets her coffee cup down and Alex and Vie are in there waited with her. He says I will put through that request for Doris and Scott I do not if it will go through but I will try. I like Doris. She has grown just in the past few days she was with us.

Chapter Seven

The next few hours brings in all the other agents of this dept. Linda sees a few new faces. They greet her and she says hello, they reply we are usually in the field on stakeouts and other such operations.

Alex says okay let us get this briefing started. Is everybody comfortable? Good we are not much closer to finding where the nerve gas is coming into the country and when. Agent King has been tireless in her pursuit of the information pertaining to this. She has built a dossier on Hans and both of his Middle Eastern contacts in the Taliban. We are going to international on this on agent Kings Advice. We need help people. We need the whole world looking for these people and keeping an eye on them. All right people get to work on your contacts. Let us see what we can bring up.

A few hours later a couple of the field agents approach Alex and says we think we have a nibble. Good let's see if it pans out. They go to the meet and they also have two other SUV's filled with Agents just in case something happens. The gut feeling Alex had come true. The meet went a little sour. They had a group of hard liners waiting for them. Five minutes after the meeting started the shooting started. It was a very good thing Alex said to wear their vests. Linda and the agents in her SUV got there first and took out most of the terrorists that had been laying in wait. Agent Harris with his team took out the rest of them and the two field agents came out with no injuries. They were also able to capture the three that set up the meet in the first place. They have been taken to a place to be questioned by the Justice Dept.

Later that day Linda gets her reports on the interrogation of the three who attacked her mother. They were Mercenary's that were paid to kidnapped her mother and just hold her. She was not to be harmed but when they saw this crazed looking naked woman pounding the shit out of them they took the next step and upped the violence level.

Agents were sent over to look at what was at their headquarters. They found some information there on the retrieval of Linda's mother. They had a small room set up to hold her. Also the where and when for the meet that had this morning, the financial records that Linda accessed showed that five hundred thousand dollars had been deposited in there off shore accounts. Linda sent a request to Alex to contact the CIA to seize those accounts and to have that money put into our operating budget.

Linda's mother and Doris were both released later that day. Linda said to Doris I would feel better if you stayed with my mother.

Those men that attacked her were not gentle. I had to break one man's jaw and dislocated another ones shoulder and the third is still having problems pissing after I knife handed him in the kidney. But they have talked and they were sent a sum of money to hold my mother for a while. No reason given and no other instructions other than she lives until told otherwise.

I would be happy to; if she is anything like you I will enjoy staying with her besides I still need to rest. Yes and both of you can walk. My mother loves to take long walks and that will help with getting your strength back. I would suggest that you get a lighter pistol for the time being until your strength returns. A small .380 or older .32 caliber pistol would be fine and you are a dead eye anyways. I sure am. They go down and get to her mother's room and the cop lets them both in after they show their badges.

The doctor is in there fixing the brace one last time. Hello Doctor Hines Linda says! Hello Linda. Your mother is one tough woman she insisted that I change the brace without medication. Mom Linda says what is going on? Well my daughter I will not have the medication when I get home and I need to see if I can endure the pain of getting dressed in the morning by myself. But Mrs. King you were told, that you need to have somebody with you at all times and the hospital has sent you several at home nurse's for you to talk to. I did not like any of them for several different reasons.

Hey Doc I think I have a solution to all this. Linda says my friend here is a fully qualified field medic and she to needs a place just to rest. Now she is a friend of a coworker and mine. She can stay with my mother and help her with all those things my mother cannot do. I know her she will accept agent Trine, and she is still under the protection of the Justice dept. Well when you put it that way I guess we have no choice. Linda says I did try to make it painless.

It was settled Doris was staying with Linda's mother and so was Jake. Linda dropped them off at her mothers and Scott stayed there until Linda could get Doris an issue weapon with ammo and a couple of vests. She also picked up her cat Jake and his food. His spare litter box was all ready over at her mother's place. She stopped and picked up more litter and drove back to her mother's place.

Scott met her out front and said everything is set up. We have the place wired, Doris has Alex's number, and mine just in case. Linda goes inside and her mother is fretting that she cannot do that much at the moment with only one arm working. Doris says just tell me what to do Mrs. King and I will do it. Linda her mother says I do not know about this. I hardly know your friends here.

Mother please sit down, I will explain. Doris is an agent in my office and this man here is an agent in the office where Doris use to work. But we help each other a lot with many different things.

Now Doris and Scott happen to really like each other. But Linda I sensed you and Doris have a deep feeling for each other as well.

Yes mother but I consider Doris like a sister. We have been together as lovers but that was just a one-time thing and sense that time we have grown together as sisters.

Well then Doris as my newest daughter come and give your mother a hug. Doris gives her a gentle hug being careful of her one arm. All right she looks at Scott come in her boy and let us chat for a few minutes. If you are going to be dating my newest daughter I want to know a few things.

Linda left them and went back down to the office and logged on her PC and the boys at Langley found some of the money trail. It is a lead to London England with the World Bank. She sends this in to Alex and asks to see if we can get something going over there with Scotland Yard and MI5.Sure can sit down a moment and take a break. Vie bring in some coffee for three, yes dear.

She comes in a few minutes later and sets down the mugs and Linda sips hers and smiles. Ah one of the few things in life worth living for is coffee and the other is love. I have coffee and I have the love of my mother and my cat and my newest sister Doris and best of all I have you two as whom I love as my dear friends. Vie says we both love you to Linda you have changed our dull little office into a place that we wish to come to work, not have to come to work. Linda says that is sweet.

While they were just taking a break the red phone rang and Alex jumped at it. He says okay trace it if you can. Alex says follow along with this! He punches a button the other phone and it goes directly to a speaker, Alex says to whom am I speaking with?

This is the spokesman for the group of people you are trying to stop, as you can see we know about your operations operative Agent Linda King. Our people we have in places you would never think of have identified her. Well we have something along the same lines to buddy. Enough of the small talk! I am here to tell you we will release the gas in thirty days time in a large American city. I also know you are trying to trace this call. So sorry you will not find us. Then they all hear the sound of a phone disconnecting.

Damn it! Alex exclaims they are getting cocky! Linda says if we do nothing they will just release the gas anyways. But who is to say. Linda stops in mid sentence and gets a shocked look on her face. She asks Alex can we find out if more of that Isotope is missing, I supposed we could. What are you getting at Linda? If that gas were also the carrier of radiation from that isotope what would the damage potential be?

Radioactive nerve gas, damn that is damn low and damn nasty. Linda says we need to warn the public in such a way as to not cause a panic. Alex says I have a suggestion. We could have the local news do a special report on that area on the East side were we found that one sample and then it would be picked up by the national news services then international. We could then have the President raise the threat rating up another notch.

Alex Linda says that sounds great. But in the mean time we still have to catch those bastards. Yes you do. So your first stop will be London England to get help from MI5 and take out some Terrorist cells there of the Taliban. Linda you and your team will be heading out in the morning and flying by military air transport to RAF Lakenheath England. I was stationed there once when I first got my commission.

Oh the crap I went through during those years! Well you will be arriving real late tomorrow evening over there and from there a billet will be provided. As to that leak Linda we have it nailed down but we are just watching it for now, we will keep you informed.

Alex says get some rest in the back room you have been up for a long time. Vie will wake you in a few hours when it is time to go. Alex but you need some sleep to Oh I will get some never worry about that. For the fore see able future Vie and I and Agent Harris will be manning the office 24/7 and teams on full alert.

Linda goes back, grabs a blanket, and sits in a recliner chair that turns out to be really comfortable. She lies back, and is asleep like a light being turned off she is so tired. Vie wakes her up about four hours later and hands her a glass of apple juice and her medication. Vie says morning sunshine! Morning yourself Linda replies. Vie says that is the last of your medication. So take it and let's get you something to eat. I know you like lots of protein so I had your mother get a dozen hard-boiled eggs sent over and I got the juice. Linda eats her breakfast while Vie fills her in on the where and when and you will be leaving within the hour.

Also your contact in MI5 will be Hamish O'Connell. He is there man who knows anything about the Taliban and Al-Qaida you meet him after you get to London, you will be traveling armed to. Alex reaches into his desk and pulls out several passports and I.D. Cards and such. He hands a set to everybody they are passports with driver's licenses and international weapons permits on aircraft and in certain foreign countries.

Everybody has a small bag with civilian clothing in it and they also have a larger suitcase for their uniforms and extra gear. They will be going over there in the civilian clothing. Linda has on her black, steel toe boots and with a black crop top, and her black fleece top over that. Over that is a combat shoulder rig for her customized colt .45 and three extra clips. The rest of the team is similarly dressed; they fly nonstop to the Royal Air Force Base and set down.

The Security police commander is there to greet them and he is nobody that Linda recognizes. He asks! Are you all armed like she is pointing to Linda? Is there a problem Major Allen Linda asks? Yes there is. You cannot come on this base with those weapons. Linda says guys as team leader I will handle this. Sense I speak perfect Air Force I think this Officer will see our way here in a minute.

The Major asks Just who in the hell do you think you are. Then Linda pulls out her badge and her international authority and then her Military I.D., Which Alex had reactivated her commission and promoted her to full Colonel. Linda says now are you going to hold us here or get in the way of us doing our duty in trying to stop a terrorist. No Mame!

Thank you Major Allen you have been a big help. Now if we could get a couple of hot meals at the officers club. I seem to remember them having a decent steak last time I was stationed here. They still do Mame!

He has base transportation take them to the special VIP Billet and then to the Officers mess for a hot meal. He does ask that if you would display your badges so the others will not ask questions. Sure and after the meal I need to brief the base commanders of here and Mildenhall.

All right at 21:30 hours I will be ready to meet them. When the time came, Linda and all nine other agents went over to RAF Mildenhall to the Base Commander's Conference room. She briefed both Commanders on the situation. Both had heard about the gang land radiation deaths. Both Commanders had the security clearance for the information so Linda spelled it out for them. The Lakenheath Commander asked Linda is that I.D. real or is it a CIA fake. Linda says it is real. I was a retired Lt.Col in the security police field and a commander of a squadron on the wing level. My commission was reactivated and I was given a step promotion. My direct commander is the chief of Staff. But I still understand the chain of command.

Where were you stationed at if I may ask if it is not classified, No it is not. I was in command of the security police on Dover Air Force Base. Now I recognize you he says. You were stationed here about fifteen years ago as a fresh young second lieutenant. Yes I was stationed here for three years. Then I moved on. But can we please get back to the briefing. My men and I are very tired and we need some decent rest before we start our mission. Now have you received the list of items we will need and a place to set up yes and it is set up as of right now, that's good commander.

Linda says I will give briefings when we can and I get the go ahead from my superiors. I will be playing this by the book. Oh and gentleman MI5 will be here in the morning and agent Hamish O'Connell. He is to have full clearance and access to both bases and once he gets here have him escorted to our compound. Thank you sirs! With the briefing done with Linda and all the agents leave and finally get to their rooms at to VOQ.

The night is uneventful and they all get to the compound. They quickly get there equipment set up and get connected to the database at Scotland Yard and Langley. Linda gets a secure line and calls the home base and lets them know about the initial briefing.

Also Hamish O'Connell should be arriving at anytime. Good work so far Linda Alex says! For now check in once a day and we will keep you informed off any changes by the satellite database setup or by secure cell phone which you should all have by now. We have them and charging the extra batteries for them as well.

See you later Alex Linda says! Later Linda just watch your six. Yes sir!

The base phone rings and it is the Law enforcement desk saying an agent O'Connell is on his way to the compound. Thanks she says. She walks out to the compounds gate guard and says my contact should be getting here any moment. Yes Mame the airman replies. Sure enough a minute later a car pulls up and the airman inspects the I.D. and salutes and the man inside returns the salute. He slowly goes through and pulls off to a parking spot and Linda steps closer and waits for him. He gets out of his car and looks at Linda and says my you are a pretty Bird now.

Thank you sir Linda says my name is Colonel Linda King of the Justice Dept. she extends out her hand and the man says well Mate my name is Hamish O'Connell. It is a pleasure to meet you as well. Linda see's that he looks a bit like a famous British actor. That one from the latest James bond films, Pierce Brosnan. He seems likeable she muses!

Let's go inside and we can get an update on the situation and see if there is anything we can do. Inside Linda introduces Hamish to the rest of her team and he says I hear you people are all top agents working in a special branch of the justice Dept. That's right Hamish and you work for MI5. Right and right again.

Hamish says here let me pull up my data I have on the terrorist cells just in this area. He pulls a list of about twenty different places on it. He says now only half of these names or places have any meaning at all. The others, the ones in blue are just to keep an eye on. In your opinion Hamish who do we hit first and drag in? Sense they have gone out of their way to say they are going to gas an American city in less than thirty days time we need results fast. So I have been authorized to us whatever means I deem necessary to get that information. That included truth serum and other drugs at my disposal.

Hamish says I agree and so does her Majesty's secret service MI6. All available agents are working on this. But this team is the lead team and here is the first place to hit. It is a pub in Sussex County in a small town.

What about spy corner over on Mildenhall. That should be watched as well. Hamish says I can get a person there part of the time. Linda says I can have the Base commander get somebody to watch it as well.

Linda says is it possible to get it set up so we can deal with that first cell today? We certainly can Linda Hamish replies.

But Linda says I need to have you get some agents from where ever you search the shipping wharfs and boats and stuff at Ipswich and a few others for large or a lot of containers being shipped to the United States. Also we need to get with some of the other countries around us that ship to the States a lot. We might be able to head off some or all the gas.

Then she has Hamish gather his information and she tells her team we will be going here in a few hours as soon as Hamish has is information he needs. Then she gets on the phone to the base at home and Vie answers. Hello Vie I need to have a few things done, but first Hamish is here and we will be starting this afternoon. See if we can get some help checking out the overseas shipping by boat and even if the gas threat is just that. They have proven that they have smuggled in radioactive isotopes before.

So I would suggest that a Geiger counter would be a nice addition to the teams in the states. We have one with us which I am glad Harris thought of. Vie says we have already started that Linda but the shipping lines we will check out. And please send a report to Alex on all your thoughts as well as all your agents and Hamish as well. Any information could be a big help. Vie you take care!

She goes out and tells the team to fill out reports to the effect of their gut feeling on anything they might think could happen or a course of action. They all send a report to their home base and a copy gets sent to MI5 headquarters and from there to other agencies around the world.

Linda says we need to get lunch and plan the operation and about an hour later head there and capture as many of them as possible, all if we can. Hamish says this bunch is a bit slippery but if we time it right we can get them. All right then what do you know about these people. General habits and such one is always on guard if not two. I have not seen body armor but that does not mean they have it. So we need to place our shots with care. We go in with pistols and our back-up will be MP5's. If they turn out to have body armor then we try to minimize the death rate.

After they have lunch and they have set up the operational plan to take them out alive. So they all have tasers set to a high setting. They will use those first with a back up alongside them with live rounds. They travel the roads there with Linda driving one SUV, and Agent O'Connell driving the other. These are special SUV's. The steering wheel is on the right hand side of the vehicle.

Sense Agent O'Connell is a natural driver for driving on the left side of the road and Linda has driven over here before.

They start their way to the pub in the town not too far away they get there and the noon time crowd has thinned out and Hamish says this is about the time the ones upstairs settle back down.

The plan is Hamish and I go in as a couple and we order a drink. By the way Hamish you order for both of us. They would peg me for an American as soon as I spoke. Right Luv you want a Guinness right then when we have looked the place over for a couple minutes. I will push the button on this, she holds up a small round object. Linda says this is a radio transmitter that has been modified to cut through most radio jammers. Like the one Herr Hans had.

They get out of the SUV's that have parked up the street behind a small grocery store and they walk up the street holding hands giving the appearance of a couple. Hamish says Linda you hands are warm. Thanks! She says with a smile. The walk up the street past the post office and they wait to cross the street at the zebra crossing. They finally get in the pub and Linda smiles at the homey atmosphere that is in here. They head over to the bar and there Hamish order Draft Guinness for the both of them. He pays for them and they go sit down.

They find a table in an open part in the back away from the few patrons in the pub. Linda says in a low voice. I had forgotten that a pub is such a nice place to be in. Thank you Linda he says!

Those of us here in Britain pride ourselves on our nicer pubs. Soon both have looked the place over and they have spotted one person that Hamish has identified as a Cell member. He is sitting near a set of stairs going up. Hamish says get your Taser ready and alert the others. She presses the button and they both get up with their drinks and go over towards the one man. Hamish says to Linda you take care of him I will provide back up.

Linda thinks that this will be a waste of good Guinness but it should do the trick. She unzips her Fleece coat and shows off some skin because she has on a crop top underneath.

The man stares hard at her and she gets closer. Linda asks the guy if he likes what he sees and he really does not have time to give an answer as she has thrown the Guinness right in his face and the Taser is out and she is firing it. The darts fly out and hit the guy in the chest and release 75,000 volts. He drops like a stone and Hamish has is pistol out and says to the patrons in there. This is a British secret service operation. Nobody move and we will be gone in a few minutes. Just stay seated and enjoy your food or drinks.

Both head upstairs Linda with the Taser out and Hamish with his Glock 17. Linda takes her vest and puts it on. They do a bounding over watch advance with a second team two coming up.

The other three teams are stationed around the outside of the pub and the Local constables have been informed of a Secret service operation taking place. Hamish says to himself this lady Linda King does not miss much. She has all her ducks in a row as the Americans are fond of saying.

They get to a corner and she peers around it and sees a guard with his back to her standing and leaning on the wall. She uses hand signals to say I am firing on one person, be ready.

She takes aim at the back of his legs. He appears to be wearing a pair of sweat pants so the darts should penetrate them. She fires the Taser at the back of his legs and the full 75,000 volts drops him and he loses the function of his bladder and piss's his himself.

They all advance and Linda reloads the Taser and quietly says I might get one shot stay frosty people. Hamish slowly turns the knob to the door and when he is ready he push's it open fast and hard and he goes in low and so does Linda. She picks her first target and fires and takes quick aim at the second target and fires. She then drops the Taser and draws her pistol and takes aim on the next person and sees that the other agent with a Taser has fired twice and dropped the other two targets. Hamish says clear in here.

They all pair up with their respected teammates and check the other three rooms and get one more pair of terrorist that was sleeping. Hamish says to Taser them as well. Linda fires at them both and they fall into unconscious. They get an ambulance to take them to the RAF Air Force base to their compound.

There they are put into cells and chained to a wall. They get to read a message that they have no rights under the terrorist information act and that there captures will be asking them a lot of questions. If you cooperate you be shown decent behavior towards them. They are left to their cells and an interpreter is there to write down any information that may be said. A search of the premises turns up another address which corresponds with an address that Hamish has as well. This one is supposed to have twice as many people in it. They go get the one person from a cell that Hamish says is the leader by all the intelligence he has on this cell.

Linda says ask him once if he will cooperate. If not then we give him the Sodium Pentothal. Linda says the guy might be so forth coming if I am there so I will be filling out the team reports and fill on the base commanders here.

A couple of hours later Hamish and another agent come in to the office they have set up and both get a large cup of coffee. We they did talk with the Sodium Pentothal but before we could stop it. One chomped down on a hidden cyanide tooth and he died foaming at the mouth. Damn it Linda exclaims! We are better than this we should not let them die. Even though they want to so badly for Allah!

Well I had better take care of this right away. She picks up the phone and speaks to the base commander and tells him the situation. A little while later the body has been taken away and the base dentist has been there to check and remove other suicide pills.

He finds two more and removes those under a sedative.

The next operation will be that night and Linda says we might lose a few of them this time. Same as before but this is a house kind of back off the road.

They all get ready to leave and they all have their vests on and weapons ready. Also they have radios with them this time for quick communications. Linda says MP5's first this is a hard site and away from the public so we can have a little leeway. About one half mile away they all get out and suit up with all black. They all check the loads in the tasers which they all have this time.

Then it is quick trip there and they see three sentries. After about thirty minutes she sees a pattern and so does everybody else. Linda says team two take out guard on the east patrol. Team one that is Hamish and I we take out the main road sentry. Team three takes the south patrol. On my mark, you will have 15 seconds so take aim. Hamish you ready she whispers. Ready Luv he replies.

He has aimed his Taser at the bloke and Linda has her MP5 aimed as well.

Then she taps Hamish on the shoulder and that was his signal to fire. She says in her throat microphone start. She faintly hears the rasp of the tasers as they fire and the men as they convulse in agony, surrender to the ravages of 75,000 volts.

Then as one unit they all advance and Linda takes a syringe out and push's it in the guy they just stunned. The sedative they are using is a very general one and will keep them sleeping for several hours. They advance on the house after the other two teams have put there sentries to sleep. Then the other three teams come up and they surround the house.

They all get ready to storm the place. They have a guy with a battering ram and he slams it into the door. It about shatters it so old. They go running in, shouting to get on the floor in English. One man brings his scorpion machine pistol up and starts to let loose with a stream of Nine millimeter death. Hamish spins and fires two quick shots at the man's head. One clip's his left ear and as the man turns slightly the other enters his right temple and the bullet exits the left side of his skull taking over half the brain with it.

Linda has her Colt .45 Automatic out and sees another one bringing an Uzi up and she fires one shot at him. He must have jumped up some because she was aiming at his fore head and the bullet hit his throat. As the bullet passed through the neck it severed the spine. It shattered all the bones in his neck as the bullet exited the back of the neck, the head about falls from the body.

She sees that several of the terrorist in this cell have been stunned as well. Linda says be sure to give them the sedative. They round up all of the cell members and sedate them as fast as possible. Only one can chew his cyanide pill and lay on the floor thrashing about. But it seems his pill was defective he only got really sick and was feeling really bad. So Linda called for an ambulance to take him to a maximum security hospital and make sure her does not die. She has Hamish assign MI5 agents to watch him.

The next few days Linda is able to go and finally work out. She has been feeling frustrated without working out. So she visited the base gym and worked out for a few hours and ran six miles on base and when she returned and took a shower and went back out to the compound. The other prisoners have talked and the dentist has taken all the cyanide pills away from them. All of them refused to speak English even though there files said they knew the language well. They were transferred to a maximum security holding and placed under 24 hour watch.

Linda said it is time we sifted through the data we have from them and their place. So the next day is spent basically reading everything they have. Then about 2100 hours that night agent Tomlinson asks what this is and he shows it to Hamish and Linda. Linda says I think it is a shipping invoice.

They should not have those. It is start and hopefully the break we have been looking for. They quickly locate where and when the shipment is supposed to leave and it is tomorrow morning and it is marked as insecticide Non harmful to humans. It even has an MSDS on it.

We need Full mop level four chemical gear. She calls the base Commander and he has the items sent over within the hour. Mean while she has contacted Alex and told him what they have found. The shipment is in Ipswich and they can get their within a few hours to stop it. Go for it Linda he says we will do what we can on this end to see if we can convince the British intelligence community help out as far as tracing that shipment back.

Thanks Alex Linda says! Linda tells her team to get suited up and ready. Then she inspects how they have their chemical gear worn and helps to fix any problems. They get on the SUV's and this time they have two British officers with the right security level drove the teams down there. They pull into the first area and park. The two officers have their own chemical Gear with them and they are on the same radio channel as the team.

They start out with a bounding over watch advance with two teams. One team is lead by Linda with five members and the other Agent Hamish O'Connell with the other four. They get to the ship and it is an older style ship that does not hold that many containers on it but there are open holds that have the containers inside them. Linda uses her satellite cell phone and calls Alex and says we are at the ship and it looks like there is nobody here but we will be careful. Take care! Linda we need that shipment stopped. And stay Frosty! Like it was 30 below! Yes sir will do!

They approach the gangway and go up being sure to keep a look out for any little detail. Linda is the first to spot a foot that is sticking out a little too far. She signals the team to halt. She takes out her Taser and has it set to the maximum setting and slowly advances. She gets to within a foot of the corner where the shoe is sticking out and it moves out and comes into full view. The man attached to the shoes is a Middle Eastern decent and he has a Mini-Uzi on a strap. He is also lighting a mini cigar. As the light from Lighter flared He saw Linda take aim with her Taser and fire right at him. He does not even have time to yell a warning as 75,000 volts takes a hold of his bodily functions and freezes them. He then falls to the deck. Linda reaches in her jacket and takes out a syringe and pumps him full of a strong sedative. He will be out for several hours.

They continue to the bridge and the crew quarters. They do a sweep through there and were able to surprise one other guard armed again with a Mini-Uzi. He too was pumped full of a sedative and tied up with plastic cuffs. Then it takes a while to search the ships holds but the finally find the containers that they were looking for. There are three of them and all have security seals and locks. They get out there bolt cutters and get ready to open after they check for any surprises.

Sure enough the bomb tech on the team sees a very tiny hair of a wire that is connected to a detonator in about ten pounds of Semtex. He quickly disarms it and removes the device and the Plastic explosive he puts a sample in a bag and says we need to get this shipped off and tested to see where it was made.

They all get there chemical gear masks on and check to make sure they have a good seal. They open the container and inside it is filled with barrels of some sort of fluid. None of it is leaking. Linda pulls out a chemical warfare tester and tests the air inside for chemicals.

It soon says there are no traces of chemicals. She takes off her mask and everybody takes there's off.

Okay let us tag these containers and seize them and I want the whole crew found and taken into custody on the charges of to transport hazardous chemicals. Just make the charges stick until we get back a sample of what is in here. I just hope this is all.

Those guards may not know much but let's get those other cells rounded up. We do not have to do all the work. As I understand it the British has a crack squad of people for operations like this. That they do Linda Hamish replies!

They pack up anything that might be a sample and Hamish calls it Scotland Yard to take the two prisoners away and he reminds them to check their teeth for cyanide. They get back to the compound and Linda says we need to get some rest.

A few hours later Linda is woken up by the phone from home base. Alex is on the line and says we have an initial results of the chemicals found in the ship. By themselves they were nasty and could kill if you if you breathed enough of it.

But combined and sprayed in the air it was a very nasty nerve agent. That after it landed and stayed on a flat surface it would form a skin on it and fool any chem. gear sniffer out there.

Good work Linda and also good work to the whole team. But wrap things up there and get the rest of those terrorist cells. The British Govt. has asked us to help them out.

Yes Sir Alex! But we still need to find Hans and those two very slippery guys. Does Interpol have anything on them yet? Yes they do and they are in Panama Canal. So you and Agent Hamish O'Connell will be going there as Tourists on a honeymoon. Alex Linda interrupts. She says I am sorry to interrupt but does he know about me and my ways she asks. No he does not. In fact he does not know about the mission yet so in between now and then he should be told.

Yes Sir Alex. Please Linda I am your friend. You have spoken highly of Hamish in your reports so he should accept you.

Later that afternoon when half the team was going out of a joint operation with the British SAS Linda calls Hamish into the one office they have and says you need any coffee or tea. Get some; we need to discuss a few things. Linda I will see you in a minute.

He comes back with a cup of tea and comes in a shuts the door. Linda says take a seat this is going to be a little time consuming. Ok Luv whatever you say. Linda says well it is funny you should say that because Sir and I do mean sir. I respect and like you as an agent and as a man. You have proven your worth to me and my agents on several times.

Hamish asks! Where are you going with this agent King?

Well this may be a bit of a shock or may not be. There is a piece in my file that was left out on purpose. Let us just say that very few people know this.

It is about my sexual preference. Hamish says don't tell me you're a bloody lesbo. I prefer the term Lesbian sir! He looks at Linda and says you are a fine looking woman Linda how is it that you do not like guys. I never said I dislike guys Hamish. I said I was a Lesbian. I did say you are a really good agent and a nice guy. There is a reason I am telling you all this. I was given a little forewarning on an upcoming mission.

You and I will be traveling to the Panama Canal as honeymooners to see if we can catch those two Middle Eastern types. We have their names and I know what they look like. In fact I know most of the international community has their pictures and the artist's sketches I had done.

So you and I will be going to the canal huh. So will you let me kiss you in public Linda Hamish asks? Only if you promise to behave yourself! I will ask you to please do so and we will get through this mission just fine.

Linda reaches into her briefcase and pulls out a file and hands it to Hamish. It is an outline of what happened to two agents on a mission to a nudist resort about a month ago. About fifteen minutes later Hamish looks at Linda and says one of these ladies is you isn't it. Yes it is! My supervisor has asked me to play the other half in a male female marriage and he felt that sense I have such a high regard for you that this would be easier for both parties.

I would see that would make for a better arrangement Hamish says! All right then so you will be all right with this. We will be sleeping in the same bed. We are supposed to be married for this mission so we will need details on each other's habits.

I will start, I love to work out and like most American females I sleep naked. But please do not get any ideas. I can assume most any role I need to. That is interesting Luv. I also sleep naked. So we should provide any seekers of our identity and eye full. As to assuming any role I can do that as well.

But first Linda let me assure you I will be a gentleman while we are there. Yes you will see my bits as we Brits say. I know what that means. So while we are on the subject let's just says I do not mind striping of my kit as you Brits say and going Rudy Nudy. Or as we Americans say naked. We can roam around on a few of the beach's there and we can play tourist. So Hamish let's talk some more and find out a few things.

Hamish says then I would suggest dinner at a restaurant near here that serves good food and a nice atmosphere. We can talk and possible find out a few things. All right Hamish we can do that. I have never been opposed to going out with a guy before. I did it a lot when I was on active duty.

Dinner went fine and Linda found out a lot about Hamish. He too was a career Military officer until he saw the chance to help his country. He marvels at the amount of food that Linda can put away. She says I have to eat this much just to keep me going or I would starve myself. But I also workout like a there is no tomorrow. I run about 5 miles a day now and I lift weights for about one and a half's hours each day, that is not counting the warm up I have to do because of my age.I am careful about that.

Linda that is impressive! Not to many ladies I know work out like that and look as good as you. They tend to get muscle bound, that is well for them and there are blokes that like that sort. I applaud them for their aggressiveness to weight training. But I could not date one. After dinner they walk back to base and to the compound and Linda turns in for the evening. Hamish says I have to check in at my base so I might hear about the mission then. Okay Hamish good night Linda says. Good night Linda!

Hamish goes to his home base in Cambridge and reports in and his supervisor does tell him that he will be on a joint operation with the American agent Linda King, you two will be posing as a newlywed couple on holiday. That is fine by me when do we start. In about a week his supervisor says. You will fly into the Air Force base down there and brief the local commander and staff. We will have a couple of agents nearby. The Yanks have given us the task of sniffing those two blokes out with Linda's help.

Thanks chief Hamish says I will work with Linda and get those two bastards. I think they are still trying to ship that nerve agent into the states. I would also say we need to talk to the Prime Minister and see if we can increase our own efforts in seeing if they have any plans for us as well. Good thinking man! I pass that along and you get some rest. Until Herr Hans is caught and his two associates taken down we cannot rest. Yes sir! Hamish said.

Chapter Eight

A week later both Linda and Hamish arrive at Howard Air Force base In Panama canal. They go through customs there on base and are escorted to the security's commander's office. Once again Linda produces her Colonel I.D. and agent Hamish produces a British army colonel one as well. Linda says Captain Wells While I can appreciate your dilemma. This is classified on a very strict need to know basis.

Captain Wells says, I need to clear you and your husband!

And you will simply have to wait. Linda also says I know my way around this base and you had better call the base commander now or do you want me to take matters into my own hands.

You do not want me to do that do you now.

Now Colonel King and Colonel O'Connell I will see to getting you set up in bases VOQ as soon as possible. Hold it right there Captain Linda says that is not what we need. We need for you shut up for one and two get us the base commander on the phone now! That is a direct order! Captain Wells says you are not in my chain of command Colonel!

That's enough Linda yells and stands up! I am a full colonel In the Air Force Captain and you just crossed the line. Anybody who out ranks you is in your chain of command. Do you read me mister? Do I make myself clear? About this time two security policemen came bursting into the room with M-16's leveled at Linda and Hamish. Linda looks at them and speaks before they even say anything.

Both were just young airman and only following orders.

She says airman this is a direct order put those weapons up right now or there will be hell to pay. Mame we are just following Captain Well's orders! She says let me show you my I.D. She slowly produces it and hands it over. The one airman looks at it and says Sorry Mame we were only following orders. Pete he says stand down she is legit and he asks is he and Hamish hands his I.D. over and the airman says Good day mate. I recognize this type of I.D. it is good.

Meanwhile the Captain has been sitting in his chair and stewing. He says to both airmen you both will be court-martialed for this. Linda breaks in and says I do not think so.

Linda says call the desk sergeant and have the duty Officer to come in here and that will be on my orders. Yes mame!

Captain Wells says just what in the hell were you thinking!

My job! What is that he says? Sense we came down here you have done nothing but jerk us around. We produce I.D. that says who we are. We tell you in a nice way we need to speak with the base Commander; you blocked us at every turn and then you had the gull to have two airmen pointing a loaded weapon at us. I am a U.S. Citizen and a Colonel in the Air Force. My Commission is active and valid.

The Desk sergeant and the duty officer both come in and Linda shows them her I.D. and her Justice dept. I.D. as well. Hamish also shows both his I.D.'s as well his British army colonel one and his MI5 one. Linda says to the duty officer. Lt. Deans call the base commander and have him come down here. He is needed on a very urgent matter. Tell him this coded phrase.

"Wild flowers have no pollen in the summer time in Alaska."

Yes Mame!

He goes and the desk sergeant asks why you wanted me here Mame! Because Sergeant I know the regulations on a matter like this. Your Captain has committed treason and he is going to get hauled off to a lock up. All will be explained to the base Commander Sergeant Thain.

The base commander does show up about fifteen minutes later and says when he walks in to the Captains office. Just what in the name of Sam hell is going on here? Then he recognizes Linda and says it is good to see you Captain. It is not Captain anymore sir it is Colonel King now and I am also with the Justice Dept. I see!

What does this have to do with calling me on a red priority to get down here as fast as possible? She explains the situation to him and he says all right Captain Wells you go to lock up for now! As soon as he said that He had been waiting quietly for the moment to strike. He whips out a very small Glock pistol that holds eight 9 millimeter bullets in it.

As he takes aim he fires once and Linda is diving for the base commander and forces him to the floor just out of site of the Captain. The bullet passes over them and smash's into the wood trim in the door and lodge's in it. Then Hamish pulls his Pistol and takes aim and fires and shots him in his hand. The pistol drops from his now lifeless bloody hand and he yells in pain. The desk Sergeant had pulled his Nine Millimeter Pistol and had it aimed at the Captain and said freeze right there sir. Stay cool and you will not get another round where it would feel real uncomfortable.

He says I will not make any trouble. Linda stands up and helps the base Commander get back up and then Linda looks at the captains mouth and she snap kicks him across the top of the head and knocks him down.

She reaches into the Captains mouth and sees the tooth that was broken open but the tablet had not yet been bitten on. She extracts it from his mouth and places it on the desk and says most likely that is a Cyanide pill.

The Base Commander says I always thought there was something about him. Well we need to see if there are anymore in his cell.

His cell the base Commander asks. Linda says not here sir! Some place a bit more secure than this. They wind up in the base conference room and Hamish sweeps the place for hidden listening devices. He finds one and He says that is a standard one you yanks use. But it is an old one and the batteries are dead in it.

All right Colonel all we were trying to do was see you and explain we have a mission down here to find a couple of Middle Eastern guys that want to release nerve agent into a major American city within the next thirty days. They also have been playing with Radiation to. Possibly! Mixing the two then they release the gas. That would be a nasty combination indeed the Base Commander says.

Linda says well Hamish and I will be undercover down her to see if we can sniff out any leads. So tonight we will need to get off base without us being seen. Possibly in the back seat of somebody's car! I will do that. I live over On Albrook Air Force Station. And I can drop you off near a good hotel.

I hope you have nice luggage with you and good civilian clothes. We did sir Linda replies!Linda says I need to call my supervisor and let him know what has happened! He is going to be ticked off.

I would be to If my mission was almost compromised. She calls Alex and tells him what has happened. He tells her that there will be extra agents on their way down there within the hour to help interrogate him and help clean up the area of Taliban In the area.

Oh and Alex could see where the leak is coming from. This guy seemed like he knew everything. I thought we had him locked down but he was a decoy. We're working on it Linda stay frosty!

Yes Sir Alex Linda replies. All right Colonel this evening when you go home Hamish and I will be in your vehicle with our luggage. That evening the colonel gets them off base well enough. He drops them off at a really good hotel in the area. They check in as Mr. and Mrs. George Howell of Dorchester England. Here on their Honeymoon. They get to their room and Hamish scans for listening devices and finds nothing.

Linda points to the window and says my dear open the windows please I feel a bit stuffy in here. As Hamish opens the windows Linda has retrieved a small tape recorder of a scripted conversation between them and turns it on, while that plays at a normal level. Both strip and get on Black skin tight night suits.

Linda straps on her .45 Colt and Hamish his Glock .45 Caliber with extra ammo for each. Both have tanto knifes and Black ski masks.

They load up with thin nylon rope that will hold a lot of weight and portable grappling hooks. Also a small laptop computer with the latest Code breaker programs installed and a very small satellite dish with an encrypted transmitter.

They sneak out off the room and make their way down the outside by the fire escape. Linda Says this is the way to the shipping docks. As she takes off in a slow jog. About an hour later both Linda and Hamish are observing a ship in the docks that is supposed to get the shipment of gas. But so far the ship remained empty.

Linda wanted to make sure so they find an easy spot to get in and they are careful and look in all the holds. They are empty. But Hamish says I can place a couple of cameras that will record 24 hours. We can downloaded it to the Laptop and check it out daily.

They place the cameras and make sure there are well hidden. Then they take both take out colorful shirts and Linda has a pair of shorts and so does Hamish. In the bushes both strip to their birthday suits and put on the festive clothing with sandals for both. They start to walk back to the hotel by way of the beach and there are still people there after dark partying and sitting together and some other things. Linda says well George my new husband as she holds his hand and they walk on the beach.

The air was warm and soon Linda says the ocean looks inviting. Hamish says too bad you did not bring a suit. Linda says I do not need one. This beach is a clothing optional beach I checked. Here hold my stuff for a few minutes. But Linda Hamish Hisses! We do not have time for this. Yes we do if we are to let anybody who is following us think we are on a honey moon. At that the shorts and shirt are off and Linda is standing there naked and leans in close to Hamish and says all right Hamish kiss me and let's give them a show. Because I know we are being watched. She kisses Hamish and it lasts for a full two minutes.

After they part Hamish whispers in her ear well Luv that was fantastic and she whispers back you're not so bad yourself. She then walks to the ocean and walks in. She swims for about twenty minutes and Linda cools down a bit. Then she gets out and says lets walk a little bit. I will hold my stuff but I need to dry off so I will remain naked for a bit. Hamish whispers to her Luv I need you to put on your clothing I am feeling like I would love to jump your bones now because you are so gorgeous.

Now George Linda says in a normal voice you will have to wait until we get back to the hotel room for that. Then she leans in and says so I affect you that way huh? Yes you do Luv! For that I am sorry sir, Linda whispers! She looks at herself and says well I have been working out a lot. She puts her shorts back on and then her shirt and carries the rest of their stuff.

They finally get to the end of the beach and get a cab and it takes them back to the hotel. They go up to their room and get cleaned up, and change for dinner. Linda wears a little black dress with nice strappy black heel shoes and Hamish has on a black suit and a tie. They go to the dining room and get a table and have a huge meal. Linda has a large Lobster with a New York strip steak and salad and steamed mixed vegetables. Hamish has a big appetite as well.

He orders a Cornish hen on a bed of couscous and wild mushrooms and they both share a bottle of the house wine. All throughout dinner both of them were careful on the amount of wine they drank.

After dinner they went back to their room and start in on the second of their scripts. They watch a movie on the TV that is there and Linda does kiss Hamish a couple of times. She whispers just in case they can see us in here.

Which would not surprise me, did you set up the jammer Hamish she whispers. Yes Linda I did and he returns the kiss. Linda accepts the kiss and a fire seems to ignite inside her from it. Linda says well luv it is time for bed and I for one do not plan on sleeping much. That was said out loud and part of the script. She stands up and goes to the Luggage and retrieves her wedding night lingerie and goes to the bathroom and changes in there.

She comes out and she has decided to hell with the lingerie and goes naked. Hamish stands there and stays well my dear wife you do seem eager. Linda comes forward and wraps her arms around him and says as part of the script. Yes my love I am, then she leans in close and says please Hamish be gentle with me. Hamish replies I will be because I respect you. With that Linda helps him get off his clothing and they both walk holding hands to the big bed in there and they get in. That night Linda experienced a very gentle type of loving from Hamish and she loved it. Hamish was a total gentleman in bed and was kind and considerate. The next morning Linda looked at Hamish in a new light. Here was a very experienced field agent for MI-5 and she was an agent for the U.S. Justice dept. She had told Alex she would do what it takes to follow through on any mission and there were people watching them last night. Even though the jammer was operating they could have been using an extended range m icrophone to listen in on their conversations.

But all they got was whispering and scripts and lovemaking. Linda got up still naked and went to the phone and ordered room service for breakfast. She said everything in a slight British accent and slang. She orders for Hamish his eggs and pancakes with lots of butter and syrup and she gets a very large omelet of five eggs and milk and a large pitcher of Orange juice.

Hamish wakes up and sees Linda and says! Well luv how are you this morning? Linda replies ready for the beach again today and I want to make sure we are not disturbed to.

So I know of a place that might be empty, that if we are lucky. But first as she gets up and goes over to him and says let me wake you up the right way and gives him a kiss that would ignite a forest fire. Hamish says well luv where did that come from?

Linda replies! From my soul Luv! A knock on the door and Linda puts on a robe and hiding her gun in a pocket. Hamish gets in the bathroom running the shower and waiting. She looks though the peep hole and she presses a speaker button and says in Spanish "Hello Can I help you. The Server girl says I have breakfast here for Mr. and Mrs. Howell. Linda replies to the young lady Linda replies in text book Spanish" She lets her in and she wheels in a cart with breakfast on it and the server says is this all Mame!

Thank you and Linda gets her wallet and pulls out a five dollar bill and gives it to the young lady and says thank you.

Hamish comes out of the bathroom after she has left and Linda has once again naked in the room. He says well luv If you do not mind and he comes to her dropping his towel and gives her another very passionate kiss. Linda response to it and she returns the passion. After about two minutes again Linda breaks loose and says let's eat Luv everything we did last night made me very hungry.

At that moment about two blocks away in a high rise building in Panama City in a rented office. Two Chinese agents are looking at the interaction between Linda and Hamish and are convinced that this is not the couple that was supposed to be coming here. There mole was wrong. This agent Linda King was supposed to be a lover of Females only! Yet last night she swam naked on the beach and kissed her husband fully naked while on the beach in public.

110

Then when they had finally placed the rifle microphone and tuned it right all they heard was the sounds of a movie and them softly whispering to each other and then she gets up and takes off her clothes and they make love almost all night. These are the wrong people. They do not show up are the right place and we had to track them down. The people who hired us are fools. We should have known better than to trust that source.

Back at the hotel room after Linda and Hamish finish their breakfast Linda says! Come to the couch and sit with me for a while and so we can talk Luv. Sure thing Luv! Hamish says. Hamish sits next to her and both their a rms around each other and they are still naked.

She leans in close and says last night was wonderful and I never want to lose that feeling again. But we are still on a mission and I have this bad feeling we are being watched right now. Hamish says are you worried they will see that beautiful body of yours.

Not that I do not mind I am a nudist remember! Yes Luv I remember.

Today we have to play tourist again and it will be all day. Those shipping manifests said for tomorrow but we can check it again sometime today. I agree Luv. Oh remember my name on these types of missions is Toni all right Luv. Yes Toni my Luv as Hamish smiles and kisses her and Linda returns the kiss. Then she moves underneath him and they make love again as her passion is fully ignited with delight!

Later on after they are once again after their morning delight. Linda and Hamish grab the laptop and the transmitter and the mini satellite dish plus some bottled water and a swim suits under their clothing and their weapons. It takes awhile to get to the beach where Linda said they could be left alone but they had to hike there a bit.

When they get there they set up and lay their towels out and see that the place has no one else there. Linda says I am going to go naked now just because I can and I believe we lost anybody who might have been following us. Hamish says Linda if you are going to be naked how are we supposed to get any work done? Easy Hamish we will not be making love or anything like that are we should not be. But sense we have the time at the moment to talk without anybody listening. I will say this. You moved me last night, you did what I asked of you and you have helped me get through a difficult time. I was very reluctant to go to bed with any man.

But I told Alex that I would just for the mission. But I have felt something last night and this morning that I have only felt with my first love with best friend Jenny. Yes Linda you did say you was a lesbian. Well now I guess I will have to rethink that now.

Do not get me wrong I still like the ladies. But if the right man comes along it is truly wondrous. Like me Luv Hamish says!

Yes like you Hamish.

So get your kit off and get naked and satisfy me again. With pleasure Luv Hamish says. About thirty minutes later! When Linda, and Hamish were well into their lovemaking on the beach. The two Chinese agents finally find them and see them from a distance. See you fool those are the wrong people. Yes the description is right. But the woman is supposed to be a lover of females only and I stress only. No our marks are not them. Come let us leave this place. I have no wish to witness such deeds being done.

About an hour later when they had finished and Linda had a big smile on her face she leans in close and asks did you see those two Chinese men watching us a little while ago. Yes Luv! Well Linda says let's keep up the charade and go get a swim. But only one at a time, we need to watch our stuff agreed! Hamish goes in first and basically swims for a little bit to get cleaned up a little bit and gets out. Linda help dry him off and put sunscreen on his naked body everywhere!

Linda gets in the water and gets herself cleaned up and does about the same thing and gets out. Hamish helps dry her off and he liberally puts tanning oil all over her naked body! They sit down on the big towels and drink some water and get out the laptop and the transmitter and Hamish downloads the cameras video images sense last night. Mean while Linda is setting up the mini satellite dish and getting it connected to the laptop. She has Hamish up-link to a spy satellite and set up a live chat with Alex at the office.

They tell Alex that there are two Chinese agents that are following them but we have tried very hard to make them believe we are who we say we are. Linda says to Alex I have found somebody I am very comfortable with as a man so that has helped us with us undercover. We will be uploading any and all videos we have to you and you can get a team on them. This afternoon we will be eating in a Panamanian Restaurant that specializes in beef dish's for a low price. Have your team meet us there and we can set up a sting on those Chinese agents. Alex replies! I know the place Charoo's right!

Right Alex and tell Vie I am all right now. I have found what I needed and send my best to Doris will do. Take care! Alex out!

A little while later they sit down. They eat some lunch that they brought with them. Linda has a couple high protein bars and a carbohydrate bar all chocolate. Alex settles for a couple of sliced cold cut sandwiches they brought from the hotel and a both drink water.

After their lunch Hamish lays down on the towel and Linda once again applies sunscreen to his entire naked body. Luv if you like to apply sunscreen to that so much! Could you at least make it a bit more enjoyable for me? Linda replies I am not willing to go that far yet. But if you want the other we can do that. Well you are not shy in that department Linda. Linda says I want to do it in the water this time. All right Luv! They get up and both wade into the ocean and soon they are locked in a very passionate lovers embrace.

Afterwards when they have gotten out and sunscreen and tanning oils reapplied did Hamish lie down on the towel and lightly sleep.

Linda takes the time to move the laptop undercover better and makes sure she can get to her Pistol. About fifteen minutes go by and Linda is wondering why she is feeling like she does for Hamish. She has known love before. But this is different. This is something she will have to talk to Jenny with sense Jenny have taken a male as a lover too Linda needed some answers.

Linda hears a noise that does not belong there and she very quickly turns with her colt in her hands and she sees two Middle Eastern men advancing towards her. Both have Russian nine millimeter Makarov Pistols and she quickly stands and kicks Hamish and hisses we have company. Get moving George and bring your friend. That was a signal to get up and grab his pistol.

About then one of the Middle Eastern agents opens up and fires at Linda. The bullets sails past her and she snap fires at him and her aim is much better. She hits him center mass and the force of the large caliber bullet as it hits him, slams through his chest and bounces off his rib cage and smash's into his heart blowing it into many small pieces out the back of him. He falls to the ground with a look of total shock that a naked woman shot him dead.

Hamish grabs his Glock and thumbs off the safety and sites in on the other Middle Eastern agent. He squeezes the shot off and his .45 caliber bullet enters the head just above the right eye, as it continues on its deadly path it exits the brain and takes with it a large chunk of skull and almost half the man's brains with is. The agent twists from the force of the bullet backwards and his feet fly up and over his head and he does a somersault and lands on the front of his body. Linda says do you see anymore?

No Hamish says finally standing! Linda says let's check the area out fast and get our suits on just in case the police show up. Agreed! They quickly reconnoiter the area and find nothing but there vehicle with the keys left in it. Linda takes the keys and says we have a way back so let's get dressed and head back fast.

They finish getting dressed very fast and get to the car and load up and they leave it fast. They do not hear the police or anything else. They get to about two blocks from the hotel and Hamish calls Alex and gives him a report and says those two most be the other half to the other two we have in our sites now. Leave the vehicle and go back to the hotel and continue to be honeymooners and tomorrow night both of you will take a trip to the shipping docks and see what's in the containers after they arrive. Got it Alex!

They abandon the rental car after they wipe it down leaving none of their prints. Then they walk back to the hotel and as soon as they walk in they give each other a very passionate kiss right at the receptionist counter for about two minutes again. Linda asks the lady for their key and she gives it to them and they go to their room. They get cleaned up for an early dinner at Charoo's.

Linda wears a short wrap around dress and sandals and she carries her large hand bag. Hamish wears light khaki pants with a white silk shirt that he does not tuck in and he puts the Glock in the waistband under the shirt.

They get a cab and go to the restaurant. Alex had sent word that the agents in the area were staying deep in the shadows and that you two are the draw or the honey for the bee. They want them to focus on you.

They have a very good meal which Hamish is astonished that Linda can eat so much. She says it is low in fat because it is grilled and all the fat goes away from the meat.

Besides I will burn all this off when I work out this evening. I need to run on the beach. Which beach you running on Toni Hamish asked? Why the one where I can run naked of course. Of course he replies! I will run with you. Thank you George that is sweet of you.

I just hope I do not throw up all this good meat while I run that far. How far do you usually run George? Well Toni I only go about two miles and then rest and then a lot of pushups and the like. Tell you what dear I will do what you do so you do not get sick and lose your dinner.

Remember Toni dear this is not a contest to see who is fitter. I will dear! They get back to the hotel and relax a while and Linda sits on the couch with Hamish and says this is nice. I have never felt so good unless I was with my mother. Hamish says well lass I am glad I could do this for you, I have enjoyed our time as well and I am getting really fond of you. But the mission comes first and we are both professionals he whispers to her.

Linda replies I know we are both professionals and we will do what it takes to complete the mission but I believe I am becoming fond of you as well. All right Linda stop right there! Hamish whispers to her. But Linda says I know we have to keep this professional, I cannot help that I am beginning to understand what a woman actually feels like when she has had the right partner.

You have been very kind and gentle with me. I also sense you would like to try other things. I am not ready for wilder sex yet. But let's have a little sex now and then go work out. That may help you.

Linda and Hamish have a mind blowing session of sex. Linda Is coming more convinced that she is falling for Hamish but she knows she needs to keep this as professional as possible. But as long as the sex is fantastic she does not want it to stop. After about an hour they untangle and get ready. Linda dresses in skin tight Hot Pink spandex short shorts and a string bikini top that match's her shorts with white Nike's. Hamish gets on red Bermuda swimming trunks and a sleeveless t-shirt and red Nike shoes. They load up with a several towels and sun tan stuff and lots of bottled water. They call a cab to take them there and the whole time the driver and most other guys were eyeing Linda because of her very beautiful body.

They finally get to the beach that they were on the first night. It is still day light when they get there and Linda says I need to still warm up even though we are still warmed up from the sex. I want to make sure. Hamish says on that I agree. The first thing Linda does is get out of her little bikini top and shorts and takes off her shoes as well. Hamish says you really like to be naked huh Toni. Yes my husband I thought I told you that.

I guess you did but I did not think it was this much. Linda replies. If I could I would be naked all the time. But my job and yours does not let that happen all the time now does it! No! Toni It does not! He starts to stretch and warm up a little and sees that Linda is really stretching and getting warmed up. He looks at this beautiful woman and admires that she is in such good shape. Toni Dear! Hamish says! How long do you warm up for, I forgot!

About a half an hour or so! Want to help me? Sure! Strip off she says. Hamish gets his clothes off and helps Linda warm up and he is getting a lesson in how this woman stays in shape.

After their warm up she starts on a slow jog on the beach bringing with her, big bag with all their stuff in it. Hamish offers to carry it. Linda says half the time we switch back and forth. All right dear Hamish says.

They run about three miles and Hamish says that's it for me. Linda says I am just getting started. I know luv but I have not worked out like this in a while. Well you were doing fine last night and this morning with stamina. I was motivated luv. I'll bet! I was you are such a beauty to behold I feel I could keep going. I supposed if we make love now you could keep up your heart rate. It is a possibility.

Men she says! Always wanting what we have. Can you blame us? No because right now I want what you have as well. There is a hiding place over there let's go. They find a small secluded part of the beach and make love again for the next hour.

Afterwards Linda says I still need something for a work out so I will swim back you carry the bag. Hamish replies just be careful out there. There are not real sharks here and I did my homework before coming here. I can swim just off shore and be fine. But we still need to watch out. You can stay naked if you want I swim better naked.

Linda gets in the ocean and swims all the way back less than fifty feet from the shore line. Hamish watches her emerge from the water and sees what looks like a Greek goddess coming out of the surf.

He says Toni! Keeping to their cover names! Do you know how beautiful you look, coming up and out of the ocean like that? Linda blush's some and still keeps to her mission and replies no George I really do not look at myself as really a good looking lady.

You my luv are and much more as he embraces her and kisses her. The fire of his passion ignites her passion again and once again Hamish and Linda want to have that passion consume them. But Linda says with a slightly husky voice we should get back to the hotel and finish this. Besides I want a shower after that salt water swim. Hamish clears his throat and says I can agree with that.

They get dressed and get back to the hotel and they did not even make it to the shower and they were just inside the room making love on the carpet.

Later after the rug burns are taken care of. Linda takes a shower alone and Hamish takes his alone. Linda does say this to Hamish as she pokes her head in while he showers. At least we are keeping up the illusion we are a newlywed couple and having sex whenever possible. Your Right luv and she leave the bathroom and went in and sat down on the bed. She then lay down and was soon asleep. Hamish came out of the Shower with towel around him and saw his mission wife sleeping and went to the mini bar there and poured himself a drink of vodka on ice. He sat there and thought about what Linda had said. She was still naked sleeping.

Hell Hamish old Bean you have never had a woman like this ever. She is so strong and caring and she is falling in love with you and bloody hell man you are falling for her as well.

He gets out the back up High frequency jammer and tunes it so that only the most advanced listening devices can hear them. He walks over to Linda and sits next to her on the bed and says hey sleepy head wakey wakey sleeping beauty!

Linda stirs from her sleep and sees Hamish and she smiles up at him and he says I have been doing a lot of thinking and I would like you to do some as well Linda As he holds up the backup jammer. She sees he wants to use their real names.

Linda says! Hey Hamish what's wrong. Nothing luv that's it nothing is really wrong. The mission is going fine and we have about convinced those stupid agents we are not who they seek even though we killed two of their agents only yesterday.

No! I have been doing some thinking and it has been on what we have been saying to each other as agents and as a mission couple. Now I know we are both professionals and I have always respected a fellow agents wish's with anything they wanted. But you are the first to affect my judgment how Hamish how have I affected your judgment? By being such a kind lady, just by being you.I believe I have fallen for you.

Now before you say anything I will be a professional and we can finish this mission. Linda sat and hugged Hamish tightly and said in his ear Oh my Hamish you have fallen for a woman that has seen only two other men in her life. I believe you when you say that you may have fallen for me. Because to tell the truth Hamish. I believe I have fallen in love with you! But like you said I need to do some thinking on this. It is not just the sex that's great.

But what of our careers You as MI5, me as a Justice Department agent?

Linda says I need to talk to a friend of mine. She has always been there for me. Hamish asks is that Jenny you are going to call. Yes Hamish it is. Thank you. I know you value her opinion like a trusted family member.

Linda calls Jenny and explains in detail the love life she has had just in the past few days. Linda does use the secure satellite phone that she has. She also knows Alex will need to be told about this call.

Jenny says I do sense a change in you my dear friend. I have seen you accept men as your boss and that seems to work well for you. I kind of figured it would only take time to find the right man. But I will warn you, Make sure he is the right man. Great sex sometimes does not mean a good man in a relationship. I will Jenny Now I am going to let you talk to him for a few minutes. Five minutes later Hamish cuts the connection and says that is one loyal friend. She said that if I find out I hurt you she will personally fry my balls and make me eat them. From what I have read she was in the Air police like you. Yes she was my trainer at first then she was my friend then my lover.I knew you had lesbian affairs before all this. Yes she was my first and I only had a few more. Then I was given a drug while on assignment in Jamaica. Even if the mark had not given me the drug I would have gone to bed with him. But sense he was a free lance agent and getting chemical weapons and such for the stock piles of the old U.S.S.R.

I went to bed with him but only after our other female agent did not get the information to. Her dose of the drug was much higher and than mine and my body's chemistry was different than hers at the time. I had a high concentration of lactic acid build up from my afternoon run and long ocean swim and from the dance contest I won.

Hamish says I know the drug but we thought there was no defense. Well there is going to be soon. This was their first break through. But anyways he date raped me and Doris the other agent with us. I was actually retching from the poison in me my body reacted so violently to it.So now you know a little about why I was so reluctant to go to bed with a man. But the big one is that I was raped when I was just a very young teen I was just twelve years old. My step father saw what I was becoming. I had developing my chest early in life and I was almost grown to this height. So he wanted me. And he had me in a most violent way.

If my mother had not showed up and called the cops I might have died that night and there was a few times I wished I was? Soon after that we moved and my mother and I got real close and she helped me rebuild my life. But I vowed to never go to bed with another man. Until that mission, and now you!

I almost chucked it all again but again my mother helped me through the pain and a shrink from the Justice Dept. I got to where I could trust a man again. Not that I did not trust Alex. He was safe he had a loving wife and a fellow agent.

Say Hamish is it possible for you guys in MI5 get loaned to other agencies? I do not know luv. Let's ask Alex besides we need to check in.

A few minutes later Linda has a robe on and Hamish has put on his shorts and a shirt. They are setting up a video satellite link.

A couple of minutes later Alex and Vie come on and they see Linda is all smiles and Vie knows even over the link what she has been doing. Vie says Linda I see you are glowing have you made a decision young lady?

Yes Vie I have but first things first we are sending in the latest downloads from the shipping docks Direct. Hamish knows how to do that and it is faster than me doing it this way. Alex I need you to please think this question though. It is important to me. Is there any way we can get Hamish assigned to your team.

Vie asks Linda I am going to have to ask you a direct question Is that all right. That is fine Vie. Have you been sleeping with agent Hamish? Yes Vie I have. I see Hamish how do you feel about Linda. Do you want the truth Vie! Yes I do. He looks at Linda and says I believe I have fallen in love with her and Linda says I believe I have fallen in love as well Vie. Alex says well is this a pickle. Well Alex I never planned this.

I know Linda I am your supervisor and I am quite fond of you because you are a good agent and a good person to be around. Hamish you are one lucky man to have a lady as Linda love you.

Linda for what I have gathered Hamish is a good agent. I will see what we can do. I will also push the paper work through for something else should you decide. I know I am speaking for you Vie says But once you both say I believe Well It is true.

It happened that same way with Alex and me. We meet on a stake out all those years ago. But that is a long story. Continue the mission and get to the ship yard tonight and plant those charges. You will get them at the prearranged spot from an old friend and he does not even know he is giving them to you. That's always nice to hear the bad guys will be losing double tonight. All right Linda and Hamish Both of you stay Frosty during the mission and come back in one piece and take a few days' vacation please! All right Alex will do.

After the link is broken Linda says well that confirms it luv I do love you and Hamish replies and so do I luv. Linda stands and throws off the robes and says I want you now on the balcony with lots of people watching! Fine by me!

Hamish says and she helps him with his cloths and out to the balcony they go and for the next two hours their passion ignites there fires within and there love grows ever more.

They explore the depths of the passion and come up wanting more. Linda has found her soul mate and Hamish has found his one true love. But will the fate of what awaits them in the next twenty five days destroy them or bring them even closer.

Later on after their wild affair in the balcony they shower together and Linda finds out that she no long desires a scalding hot shower. Then they pack there black skin suits in her large hand bag and he has a small back pack which hangs off one shoulder. Linda is dresses in a short pull over dress with sandals and Hamish is in Khaki shorts and a green tank top with sandals as well.

All the equipment is with them and they walk to a rental agency and get a sub-compact car. Linda drives to the arranged spot and sees the two big brown attaché's there and gets out and gets them. The whole time she does this Hamish has is pistol ready and so does Linda.

She retrieves them and puts them in the back seat. Then they make their way to the shipping docks and park in a secluded place.

They get out and remove their clothing and slip in the black skintight night suits and gear up with thirty Semtex charges each, and they both have lots of ammo should they need it and, a radio ear piece for both. Linda kisses Hamish and says please be careful Luv I do believe that Alex is pushing through a marriage license for us and the answer Luv Linda says in a very thick British accent, Is Yes Luv I will marry you for better or for worse.

Well I had not worked up the nerve yet but Luv I was going to ask you. And yes I will for better or worse. And he kissed her back and they went to the ship to plant the Semtex charges to get rid of the extra nerve gas that was found there.

Both of them have on the diver's footwear. The black neoprene provides a good footing and is comfortable to wear. They both proceed to the one break in the fence and slip though. Linda heads to the shipping containers and Hamish heads to the shipping office to hack into the computer and get all the shipping manifests.

Linda makes it to the Containers and sees two guards there. Both are holding Czech made Sub-machine guns that fire about five hundred and fifty rounds a minutes. Linda watch's them for a few minutes and sees a pattern develop. She whispers into her throat mike and tells Hamish she has two to dispatch. Right Luv stay frosty is the only reply she gets.

She creeps forward and slips out her Tanto knife and waits for the first one to walk by where she had creep up to. She smells the stink of tobacco as both of them are smoking and walking about. She says to herself. Well smoking will not kill this day but I will.

As the pattern suggested they come close and then part and walk back the other way. As the one guard walks by her she comes up behind him and stabs the knife in the back of the head at the base and thrusts upwards. She places her hand over his mouth for control and so he would not scream. She moved the blade around slicing up his Grey matter making him an instant rag doll and quite dead. She drags him back to her hiding spot and grabs his machine gun and both extra ammo clips.

Hamish gets to the shipping office and sees that is all dark and locked up. He slips his lock pick set out and has it opened in less than thirty seconds. He enters the office and makes his way to a bank of older computers. He touch's the key board on one and the screen lights up. Hamish is really good at reading Spanish and the whole database is in Spanish.

He starts the search for what he wants and goes to the filing cabinets and picks the locks on those and flips though the files on them. He finds the ones he wants and goes to the copy machine there and sets it up to copy every page. Next he goes back to the computer and tells it to copy all the files on the search to one file folder and compress it.

He then hooks up his small laptop computer and hacks into the main frame that way and downloads the compressed file, then he erases all traces of a search and copy's and transfers. He unhooks the small Laptop computer and gathers up all the copies for the copier. Hamish then puts the manifests back and secures the filing cabinets again and wipes the area down. Last thing he does is pulls out a regular floppy disk and puts it in the main computer and access it and types in execute.

He just started a memory eating virus that will write all ones in every sector on the hard drive and then twos and then fives and lastly zeros.

Mean while Linda has readied herself for the next guy. With her wearing no body armor she has to be careful. She peeks around the corner just as the other guy is coming around the corner. She sites in with her .45 colt pistol braced on the edge of a shipping container. She fires one shot and the large 230 grain semi-jacketed hollow point hits him just below the nose and plows through his upper jaw. The bullet continues on its flight of destruction towards the spinal column where it shatters the 3rd and 4th vertebrae severing the spinal cord. The man crumples to the deck emptying his bowels and bladder as all motor control vanishes.

Linda goes to the container and quickly exams the locks and sees they are just standard key types. She opens the radio and asks Hamish did you hear my one shot. Only slightly Luv! Well I do not want to chance it! Get here fast and we need to cut this lock and get a look inside and pictures.

She looks on the paper work on the side of the container. It has the exact same MSDS that was on the other ones! Hamish shows up and says well Luv I have all the other information from their computers. He takes out a small compact set of bolt cutters and cuts the pad lock taking another look at the set up making sure there are no surprises. He fines a small hair fine wire at the bottom and snips it.

Then he opens the door and sees that the wire would have set off a small canister of gas. It is labels as a Bio hazard In Russian. Damn Linda says! She takes pictures of all the contents and it is just about the same set up as the other shipment. She sets up the Semtex charges on all the drums and on the walls and ceiling of the container.

Hamish sets his charges up on the outside of the container and on several of the surrounding ones as well. He exams Linda's handy work with the blade and the gun shot and muses to himself to never piss her off.

They finish up and close the doors to the container and walk away quickly. Then when they get back to the car they strip off their black skin suits and once again put there other clothing on. Hamish pulls out the laptop and sets the cameras in the area to down load now to the satellite link. Then after a short wait of five minutes. Linda says well nobody heard my gunshot but in just a few minutes we need to be on the way.

Hamish says I have an idea Alex said to take a few days off. I have a friend that owes me a favor. I will send him a quick e-mail and see if he would lets us stay at his one place for a few days. Sound good to me she says. Hamish sends the e-mail to his one long time friend. The one person who a owns British private airlines! Within two minutes he gets a reply to his e-mail and says Sure thing mate I will send my private jet to the Air base there and they will pick you up and fly you there. Thanks Hamish!

He then sets the timer in the laptop for 45 seconds on the Semtex charges. Hamish says it should be a good light show but we need to be father away when we set it off.

Linda says I know a good place and there might be lots of people around. They drive to the wharf about a mile away and there is a small night club that has outdoor dancing and a small bar. They pull up and Hamish presses the execute key and the powerful laptop sends the signal to the cameras to do a live recording and upload to the satellite and to both MI5 and the Justice Dept.

Also the next signal goes out to the radio controlled detonators on the Semtex charges. They both get out of the car and look that way and the light show from the explosion is quite good. Hamish says we have time for one drink and we need to get back and pack and leave. I agree says Linda.

She gets a Local beer and Hamish gets Vodka on the rocks. They sit close to each other no longer having to pretend they are a very loving couple.

But they hear sirens in the distance and they looks at the TV above the bar and there command of Spanish is quite good so they understand the breaking news that a terrible explosion has happened on the shipping docks. It looks to be a three alarm blaze for now. Hamish says well dear lets head back to the hotel and stay out of their way. Sounds good to me Linda replies!

They make their way back to the hotel go up and pack what little they have. Then they go to the desk and tell the desk clerk they have to leave now because I have been called back to my company in England to come back and meet with the board of directors. Okay sir this will only take a few moments. Linda says we had rented a vehicle earlier today can we leave the car keys with you. The clerk said we would be happy to. Linda tells the Clerk to call a cab for us and she hands Hamish a non traceable credit card to pay for everything.

She signs it along with an itemized account of what they used. They gather their bags and go to the front of the hotel and the cab shows up. She tells the cabby the address and pays him a fifty to forget you saw us. He replies! Yes I understand. I never saw you and he holds his hand back and says my memory needs to be a bit cloudier. Hamish reaches in a pocket and pulls out the two twenty dollar bills and hands them over and Hamish says Amigo there will be only pain if you still have a memory after all that. Yes sir he replies!

He drops them off and they get there bags and they walk the last half a mile to Howard Air Force Base. They get to the gate and she and Hamish both produce there Military I.D.s and tell the Airman there that they need a ride to the visiting Passenger airlines. Yes Mame he replies! They wait at the front gate for a little while, and base transportation arrives and they get transported to the airport on base. Once there they get inside and there is a base security police detail there. Linda senses trouble but the Technical Sergeant in charge says welcome Colonel King and Colonel O'Connell.

We are here to make sure you depart with due haste. The Panama Defense Force is looking for two people that are close to your description. I have been briefed on your situation and have being taken care of by a man called Alex and his man Harris.

You also need to log on to you secure net connection and see an e-mail that was just sent to you. That's all I know. Also your transport will be here shortly, it is on final approach as we speak. There is a private room this way. The sergeant tells the detail to secure the outside of the building and that nobody comes in other than the base commander and me.

They go into the small office and set up the uplink and retrieve the e-mail. It is from Alex. It says that the nerve gas has been confirmed to be destroyed and a job well done. Take two days off and go to where you were going to go I have cleared it. I know you two will enjoy your self's. Then both of you hurry back here there are some details we need to finish then the big push will start. Enjoy Alex and Vie.

Are you going to tell me where we are going yet Hamish? No not yet Luv. It is a surprise. This had better be good to keep me is suspense like this.They pack up their gear and go out. The technical sergeant is standing next to a man in a civilian flight suit and he has a sign that says the O'Connell's. Hamish says I believe our ride is here. He grabs the bags and she carries the back pack with the other stuff in it. They get out to the private jet and it is a very nice sleek one. Inside there is a stewardess and says we will be taking off in a few minutes and says let me help you with your luggage. It all gets stowed away and the stewardess produces an MI5 I.D. and says welcome Colonel King and Colonel O'Connell.

I am agent Fiona; I am to debrief you before your two day break. Boy Alex does not miss a trick does he Hamish says. Oh and hello Fiona It has been a long time sense Basic training yes Hamish it has.

She sets out a basic cold cuts tray and a couple of bottle of ice cold fruit juice and a pot of strong coffee on to brew. Linda says I am starving and digs right in and Fiona says come on Hamish tuck in there is a lot there. Get on with it. So between mouth full's of good solid food and cold fruit juice to wash it down they are full soon enough then Fiona cleans up and Linda grabs three big mugs and pours hers and asks Fiona how do you like your coffee. Real cream and no sugar please. Hamish say black no sugar Luv.

Linda comes back and sets the steaming mugs down and she sits and says let us get started. After about an hour or so the debriefing was done and no detail was left out. Fiona says to Linda, are you sure you want to leave the love making in the report. Oh yes. We had to making it look real and I want the record to show we did our part.

All right but some of the higher ups will look at this. She looks at Hamish and says some agents I know have had notations added to their records because of this and when review time comes around they were usually passed over for promotions and special assignments. Also I would like to add a personal comment that I hope you an agent King will be happy Hamish! I believe we will be Fiona and thank you. Okay hold the phone Linda says, what is that all about? Well Linda She was my first wife, as you can see she is still a good friend and is only looking out for you and me.

That is right Linda I would imagine that your supervisor would do the same to you. Oh do not be too sure Fiona but the concern is much appreciated. You can amend the report for Hamish if you wish, it would not bother me. Alex all ready knows what we have done for the mission.

Linda says Hamish I hope that time number four is it for you! Me to Linda Hamish replies. Fiona says time number four! Yes we will be getting married in a few short weeks. Married Fiona says, you two getting married! Are you preggers or what? No we love each other and that is all that matters. Well Linda and to you as well Hamish I wish you all the best.

After my second husband I swore off men I am a lesbian now. Well it is a small world I was a lesbian before the mission. But I had decided to go through with anything as long as the other man was gentle and special. I found both and more in Hamish. Aye he is a good man. It was me mostly that caused our break up. Hamish says please Fiona that is in the past, we are still good mates right? Aye that we are!

Well it is settled when we have the wedding you are invited. I will have you as one of my bride's maids, please! All right I have some leave coming up and we will work it out. A couple of hours later they land and taxi to a remote part of the runway and Fiona says the second part of your trip is here. It is a helicopter. Linda asks where we are going. Not yet Luv. Fiona hands them a big basket of food and says I was told to give this to you. There is no food at this place this time of the year. That's all I know. All right dear and thanks!

The get in the helicopter and it takes off and heads out over the ocean in a north east direction. After about an hour the helicopter approach's a small island and says over the head sets. Here we are I will be coming back it two days time from the time I lift off. So enjoy your self's and the pilot says to Hamish a word from your friend any time pal and I expect an invitation. If you see him here is my reply you will have it mate.

They set down and they get their luggage and food basket and everything else. After the pilot leaves Hamish says well Luv here we are this is a very private island. It is owned by a very good friend of mine. He has even let special things happen on this island like a swim suit special photo shoot and a couple of men's magazines have done a photo shot here as well. This island has nobody on it. Only two ways here three if you want to swim two hundred plus miles. By helicopter or boat!

As soon as he said that Linda had her clothing off and kissing Hamish. She said this great now off with your kit luv. All right just a minute.

He finally gets naked and they make their way to the main house. Hamish sees the time and says I am about beat I need some rest we have been up almost twenty four hours. I suppose your right But once in the sun and I will sleep to. So they put the food away and left their bags where they were at and went outside in the sunshine and made love for about an hour. Hamish says Linda please we have the next two days to get caught up I am very tired. Well Luv you should sleep good now. They went inside and crawled on top of the large sofa and snuggled together and fell asleep.

Several hours later Hamish wakes up to the smell of coffee and bacon and eggs and toast. He gets up and there is Linda fixing him breakfast naked. He comes up bend her and encircles her trim waist and kisses her neck and says now this is one way to kiss the cook.

She then turns around and says this is the way the cook returns the favor and she gives him a kiss that is sure to ignite the fires of passion.

She says let go I do not want to burn the food. We only have just so much. I did make sure to tell him you have a very healthy appetite. It looks like it will be enough but just only! That's fine luv we will make do. After breakfast the clean up and go exploring the small island. Linda stays naked and so does Hamish. Linda even puts sunscreen on Hamish and he puts tanning oil on her.

Over the next day and a half they get to know each other very well. There likes and dislikes. Linda is also having a lesson in love making as well. In the ocean and on the many beaches there and in the bungalow that is there. They do have solar power so they are able to tell Alex and Vie where they are and Alex says the paper work is done and waiting on you here.

Oh and Hamish you will be transferred to me for a one year loan to get to know how us yanks work. Talk to you soon. Alex and Vie.

That is fantastic Hamish It sounds like you and I can get married almost as soon as we get back. It will be an informal wedding.

But I want Fiona there she is a good friend. She will be there if I know her. She was a little special to you wasn't she. Yes Luv she was. She and I were married for about 7 months but she could not handle it when she was told she might have to sleep with a man to distract them. She was outraged that she would have to do that while married to me. So they basically threw her out of that section and we later divorced on very friendly terms. I help when I can. We have even been on several missions together but by then she had sworn off men all together. But I was a safe one to her and we remained good friends.

So you would not mind if I kiss her at the wedding reception. He looks at her and kind of stammers and Linda says Luv I will always love you but I was a lover of female for a very long time. It would mean a lot to me to give this to her as a gift. Besides you will get to kiss my very best friend Jenny. She is as good as I am at kissing.

That would be wonderful. So later that day they did not have much to do but lay around and sun tan naked and make love almost all day. That night Linda and Hamish both slept real well.

Again Hamish was woken up to the wonderful smells of breakfast and a still very naked wife to be. He kisses her good morning and she returned the favor.

After breakfast they wondered the beach for a while made love once again on the edge of the sea with it washing over them at times. In her mind she thought that it could get no better than this a good man to love, and a deserted Island, good food, plenty of hot wild sex.

A few hours later, they have comeback and Linda has spent the last hour cleaning up. She says to Hamish that I have always done this. I straighten up and clean up after myself when I visit a palace where I stay. Except a hotel room and I classify this as a resort. Yea he likes it here. He told me one time that if I ever wanted to come here was all I had to do was ask and if it was not booked it was mine. I got a little lucky on this. But I also told him that I would only ask for this place if I had a wife or a wife to be.

So he is going to be at the wedding huh! I hope so! I will call him and Fiona when we get back and get them here. I need to get Jenny there as well.

Well I hear our ride coming so you had better put on some cloths! Oh I wish I could stay naked! So do I Luv but back to work we need to go. Yes and Herr Hans is going down! Linda gets her short dress back on and they carry their luggage out to the helicopter pad. After the take off the pilot goes back to the Bahamas Airport and again at the end of the runway is the same jet waiting on them. As Linda looks she sees Fiona smiling at them and waves. She waves back and they get on the sleek jet. Fiona hugs Linda and Hamish and says welcome back how was your stay if I have to ask.

A deserted island with nobody else around I bet you two had a lot of fun. You could say that Fiona Linda says.It is a good thing we have seen you right now. Sense Hamish and I are getting married I still want you as my bride's maid. All right Linda I will be there. But I have only a few days off before I have to be back then it is settled.

After they take off Linda gets on the Satellite phone and wakes up Jenny. She tells her I am getting married in just a few days and I want you there as my maid of Honor. Jenny says well I see Hamish has finally got you to see the way it is supposed to be.

I was hoping he would be the one. Well you are coming right. You could not stop me. I will be there by tomorrow night and I want to stay with your mother if I could. You might have to sleep on the floor because we have help there right now. That's fine do not worry we will get through this. Yes we will and she says good bye and tells Hamish I love you with all my heart and I love you Linda with all my heart. Fiona smiles!

Chapter Nine

They land In Andrews Air Force base and are whisked away to D.C., they are not told what is there, but Linda asks are we going back to our headquarters. Yes tomorrow you will be going back there. But the main debriefing will be here. But we have already been debriefed. By an agent of MI5 we know of that debriefing we wish to see if you want to add more to that.

All right! But it has been a long trip and I am really hungry and need to use a bathroom. Food will be provided at the debriefing site and a bathroom is right around the corner.

Around the corner Linda sees that there are six openly armed female agents and her senses are on full alert. She turns to the one telling them everything and asks? What is the meaning of this? I am a duly swore member of the Justice Dept.

Just hold on a second Mame! We told that you and your boyfriend here pointing to Hamish were dangerous. By whom Linda asks. By a reliable source the agent says! I want to know that name NOW Linda says! By whose authority he asks. Mine Linda says!

You do not have that clearance agent King. Hamish points out that if I am expected to go in there as well, there will be hell to pay. I am a British national and you do not want an incident. Oh there will not be one Agent O'Connell. He says! Now move along or we will be forced to get unkind. Linda says what we have done to deserve such treatment. Hamish says Luv do not give them anything. Somebody else is pulling their leashes and wants us out of the way.

About then the door on the end of the hallway where the six fully armed agents that are with Alex as comes bursting through with agent Harris and twenty Marine's all fully decked out with Kevlar and M-16 rifles. He bellows at the one agent and says Answer the Agent King! Agent Dean. Or are you just scared to admit that one of yours is the mole we have been trying to find for the past two months. Linda sees that he is sweating and the Air Conditioning is on full blast in here. It is a little cold. Then she sees him working his mouth and Linda moves forward very fast and punches him as hard as she can in the solar plexus.

He falls down to the floor trying to draw in a breath. Alex says what was that for Linda? She says let's just see his teeth. She kneels down and pries his mouth open and looks in there and sees that he had got the cap off the tooth but she had hit him just in time. She says he has a poison tooth Alex. She reaches in and with nimble fingers pulls the capsule out. She says we need something to put these in. Harris pulls out a small bag and says her Linda. Thanks Harris!

Then a shout down the hall way where the marines were there guarding the female agents. Two drop to the ground and start to froth at the mouth and convulsing. Linda hangs her head and says what a waste of human life.

She looks at the one agent she felled and says you will talk and tell us everything we want to know. Alex says we know quite a bit now but the head of their operation is somebody we cannot pin down.

Marines take those other ladies in for questioning. All though it is my guess they had no idea there immediate supervisor was a double agent.

All right Linda you want to ride back with me. All right I could use the time to debrief you informally. That would be fine Linda. They leave Agent Harris to take care of any loose ends there and head back.

Alex asks Hamish so Hamish how was it working with Linda. It was a pleasure sir. She is a bright and a very capable agent. It did not hurt that she is easy on the eyes.

Hey I resemble that remark Luv Linda says! Alex says I agree but Linda I would like to know how you decided to change your mind. I though you liked only females.

I did Alex and I still think they could be fun. But I think that if I am to be married I should try like hell to be faithful to my husband.

That my dear agent King will be a little hard, if the agency ask you to seduce somebody. But we can put in your file that you do not like to do that sort of thing. I know I was the one who started that program. It is usually single personnel that are asks to do that. But this clause will stop them from asking most of the time.

All right now Hamish it is set that you will be assigned to my office for one year and after that I can extend it for another year or two. Linda says we could have a solution worked out by then Luv. Yes we could!

Linda leans over and gives him a deep long kiss and Alex clears his throat and says Linda you certainly have gone back to being a normal woman now. Almost Alex I still enjoy kissing a good looking woman. But only if I get permission from my husband to be! Hamish says I may give it I may not, depends on the situation. But she will have permission with two already for the wedding.

Jenny with be one and Fiona will be the other. Jenny will be here tonight and Fiona will be here tomorrow evening. Linda says I could ask that this be a naked wedding but that maybe too much. My mother would not mind and Jenny would not. I do not know about Fiona and you Alex or your wife. My mother knows a Justice of the peace who is a nudist He could marry us.

Well it is summer time and the weather will be great for the next several days. You could have an outdoor wedding.

Hamish speaks up Linda I think Fiona would jump at the chance to be naked at a wedding. We will just have to ask. Alex says please if there are going to be that many beautiful naked ladies there I may not be able to control myself. Well Alex for you we will think real hard on that. The next few hours goes quiet as the drive back to the headquarters. Alex pulls in and says Hamish where do you want to stay. Alex sir I am going to marry Linda and we have been involved with each other.

Alex he is coming home with me. I assume my apt. is cleaned up now. Yes Linda we used an agency that uses all ladies as there staff. They get a ride over to her mothers and Hamish says I hope your mother will like me. I know she will. Hamish you have been good to me that counts for something in her eyes.

They get there and Linda's truck is in the drive way and Linda spots something new. A very tall fence is around the back yard and Linda smells a charcoal grill going with something cooking on it. Linda says I do believe my mother is expecting us.

They knock and then enter and Doris calls out come on back were about ready for dinner. Linda and Hamish both walk back and Linda has a Flying Doris in her arms kissing her cheek saying welcome home sister mine and is thisthe dashing new man?

Yes Doris it is. Linda says if she wants a kiss it is okay by me.

Besides I want one to. Doris Kisses Hamish but not too long and then comes to Linda and kisses her about the same and Linda asks so how you feeling all the radiation poisoning gone. Yep and your mother's arm is about all healed. She just needs therapy for it. Where is she? Right behind you young lady! Linda whirls around and picks her mother up and boldly kisses her and hugs her and says I have missed you mom.

Well young Linda I have missed you as well. So is this the pretend husband you had in that one place I could not know about. Yes mother. We had to make like we were newlyweds! I see said Linda's mother. Well come over and sit down. Doris could you get, your intended to put the burgers on the grill now. The corn can wait for few minutes anyways.

So Linda her mother asks! I have only heard a few things from Alex and most of all I only heard from Vie that you were glowing. That I can see for myself. That glow comes from a deep love for a person. I know I had that once or twice in my life.

Who is it Jenny or some new girl. No mother I need to say that while on this past mission we were watched very closely. So I made the decision to let a man in my bed with me. I had discussed this with Alex beforehand. Even after that Pig of a man had date raped me and gave me that awful drug. With the help of that good head doctor and your help mother and the help of my sensei I found my peace to a point.

I said to Alex I would only if the right man was there and could be gentle and understanding. Well the British sent Hamish here to help out in England with the problems over there. He was a huge help in clearing out the Taliban cells. His knowledge of such operations was impressive. But the Intelligence division over there or one of their superiors did not like Hamish. So they assigned him to the next joint mission. I was assigned by Alex and I did not mind sense I knew he was a good man to work with. Little did I know that the cover story that was leaked out by the Ministry of defense over there was we were newlyweds on holiday.

As newlyweds we had to be holding hands and doing things that newlyweds did in public. So we went to the beach and did a little shopping and did our operation like we were supposed to do. Hamish was a real gentleman though the whole thing. I was getting to like the attention. That's news to me Luv. Let me finish Luv Linda says.

That night on our way back we walked along a nude beach so I removed my cloths and took a quick swim. I got out and I sensed we were being watched. I was right on that. But we had to still make like newlyweds. So I kissed Hamish while I was still naked and I felt something stir deep inside me.

139

No it was not lust but it was something else. A bond was forming. As we walked along the beach me still naked and I was holding his hand the bond grew. That night after a nice dinner and a couple of more passionate kisses we watched an old movie and cuddled. I just now realized I liked that with Hamish. I know we were supposed to put on a good showing. We even had a scripted tape for a night in bed. But I went to the bathroom with my lingerie and I decided that sense he had already seen me naked and I was supposed to be his wife I could sleep naked in the same bed. But then as I walked out of the bathroom I came to him and we embraced for show and deep down I knew that we would have to put up a real good show for it to be believed.

We started to kiss and then I whispers in his ear please be gentle with me. From that point on I started to fall in love with him farther and farther.

Her mother asked so it was the sex that did it. No mother I do not think so, Hamish has been a total gentleman though this whole mission we were on. Yes we had sex and a lot of it. I am not ashamed of that I actually enjoyed it. Thanks Luv Hamish says and I will say this, your daughter is one real nice lady. Her manners and just her being a kind person has helped me I never knew could be helped.

Well it seems that you my daughter and Hamish will be getting married. Now when is the big date? That mother is something else we need to discuss. Over dinner the burgers are ready Doris's boy friend says coming inside with a very large platter of burgers. Everybody goes to the kitchen and Doris has helped set all the buns out and condiments. Linda get three burgers herself and puts catsup on two and honey mustard on a third and gets three ear's of Indiana sweet corn.

They go out to the back yard and Linda says this is such a nice place mom and such a high fence. Well you know I like to go outside naked just like you. Hamish replies so that's where you got the urge to run around naked all the time. Linda says you could say that is so.

Linda's mother says nobody can see in and the fence is a nice and solid one. Doris and I have sunbathed nude out here several times.

Linda asks how is your arm now mom. Doris says she is supposed to have it in a sling but if she sits still I let her just rest it.

Oh Linda thanks for the piece you loaned me I am now a dead eye with it and I take it where ever I go! You're welcome. After dinner Linda and Hamish help Doris clean up and then they go outside and sit down with fresh brewed coffee and Linda says that the wedding will be in a few days. It will be an informal affair. So informal, that I have thought about having a nude wedding. The guys do not have to get a tux and we do not have to get wedding dresses. Alex is only a little bit against it. He says all the beautiful naked ladies there will make his lose control of himself. Linda's mother says I have always wanted you to get married to a woman or a man that it would be a nude wedding.

Let me talk to Vie and see what I can do. We can get a couple of more guys here as well. I know all the guys down at the agency would come but I do not want them here just because I am naked. At the reception is fine. I don't expect gifts. In fact we should not get any.

All right we are having a nude wedding and Mother I assume that the back yard would be fine for a place to have it. Why I cannot think of a better place. Me neither mom!

Later that evening they drive over to Linda's apt. and Jake leaps from the floor into her arms and pushes his head under her chin hard and a lot. Purring really loud, Linda hugs him and kisses his nose and says to him I guess you misses me Huh lover boy.

She walks in still holding him and Hamish walks in and closes the door and Linda turns and says well I did forget to tell you. This has been the only steady male in my life. His name is Jake. She brings him closer and Hamish says I have always loved cats. There free spirit and total love for their pet is awesome. Yes Luv they see us as we are there pet. Not the other way around. That is an interesting way of looking at it.

She hands him over to Hamish and Jake instantly likes him. Linda says this place is small but it is quiet. In that case we can have some fun.

141

Linda smiles and says that is a certain thing husband to be. She says come this way the bedroom is back her.

Wow she exclaims the cleaners did a fantastic job here. How's that Linda? Well this apt. was ransacked before I left for England and I never was able to get back till now to see what I could do.

But Alex took care of everything.

Luv Hamish says it sounds like Alex is a very good man to work for. Oh he is Hamish he really is. She turns to him and says Put Jake on the bed please. All right Luv and after he does Linda steps forward. She kisses him long and deep. The fires of passion are once again ignited and they cannot keep their love contained. They set it free and ride the waves of their love all night long.

That next morning Linda wakes up to the smell of cooking in the kitchen and walks out there and Hamish is naked and cooking. She sees scrambled eggs and toast and he has some bacon frying up. She comes up behind him and says why thank you sir.

If you want my lady Hamish says I will serve you in bed. Linda says I would rather have you in bed but I am starving and I need to really work out with a five mile run. The sex is great but I have noticed my stamina has going down just a tad.

Not from where I am standing Hamish says. Well let's eat and we can both run and go to the weight room and head to the office. For some official reports and the marriage license and blood test.

After breakfast they do head back to the bedroom and make love once again.

Then after that Linda gets dressed in her running tights. Hamish says those look almost illegal there all most see through. Linda smiles and says I bought them because of that. I do like to be naked as you know. We will have to work on that for you.

She says! That's fine, but let's gets moving. Hamish gets his running shorts on and a tank top and Nikes. They head out and do a normal Linda warm up and they run about three miles and Hamish stops and Linda says I want to do another two miles so head over to the gym and I will meet you there.

Hamish is in the gym no more than ten more minutes and Linda comes back with her cheeks all red and flushed. She says I sprinted the last two miles. While she catch's her breath Hamish sets up the weight machines and starts a set. Linda spots for him. He is stronger than Linda but Linda has never gone for total muscle size just solid tone.

When she had her breath back which did not take long Linda says all that sex did help with my stamina. I have not lost any at all. They help each other with their weight sets and after about one and a half hours they are back at her apt. getting a shower together and having fun doing that.

Next thing they get dress for the office and go there. Hamish is giving his official I.D. and Gold Badge and he is assigned directly to Alex as his supervisor. Vie welcomes Linda back and pulls her aside and wants all the juicy details of their romance.

Later that day a call comes from the airport and it is Jenny she is there and needs a ride. Vie says go and get her and bring her here she can stay here until it is time to go home. Oh she is staying with Alex and me at our place. Oh that's wonderful she will not be a bother I promise. Oh do not worry Linda. I want the company and I dearly love Alex, but I want some girl talk to sometimes!

Linda leaves and goes to the airport and waits for her in the baggage claim area. She does not want to push the whole cop I am better than you thing in the public eye. Linda is wearing a smart looking gray pair of pants with thin white stripes and a pair of strappy heels and a gray female tank top with the same white stripes she has a jacket for it but the weather is hot. But her gun and shield are on her waist and she has them covered up so as not alarm the public.

Jenny gets there and Linda gives her a one armed hug and says I am still on duty. But it is too hot for this coat.

Jenny says well Hun! I always hoped you would be successful and you have made it.

I am very happy for you. They load her bags in the black SUV and head back to the Office. Linda says you will be staying with Alex and Vie. She wants a little girl talk and it is with you and possibly with Fiona as well. Who is Fiona? She is Hamish's first wife. I meet her and she is a real nice lady. If I had not meet Hamish I could have had a love affair with her she has been a lesbian sense her second marriage failed.

She is going to be the other bridesmaid. You will be the maid of honor. Alex is giving me away. She is happy for Hamish and the two are still good friends.

One thing this whole wedding! We will all be naked. Oh good I have always wanted to go to one. Well we have a best man it is Hamish's friend from England who let us stay at his island resort. We were all alone there, it was fantastic.

They get to the office and they go in and Linda takes her to meet Hamish. He looks at her and picks her up in a big bear hug and plants a kiss on her lips and pulls back and says in a very English accent Well Lass it is good to meet you.

It is good to meet you as well Hamish. From what my friend has said you have demonstrated you really changed her life around.

Vie comes in and says well It seems I have the dishonor of breaking the news to my husband he will be naked But the honor of giving you away. Want us in there Vie Linda asks? No I need to do this by myself. All right

Hamish asks Jenny so you and my Linda were lovers at one time. Yes we were Hamish and she has always been there for me as I have always been there for her. That is very nice to have a friend like that.

The guy coming to be the best man is almost that good of a mate but I would not have had a love affair with him. No silly you are not a gay man. I was a lover a females for most of my life.

Alex comes in and looks at Linda and says you are determined to have this wedding the way you want right. Yes and I want you to give me away sense I do not have a father you are the best man for that job. Oh the things I do for my people. First Harris needs a best man at his wedding a few years ago. And Vie needs this and most of my agents need that but Linda you have the strangest request of them all.

I will do it but please be nice to me. I will sir you know I always will be nice to you. I know, get with Vie I am wearing sandals to this after all. Fine By me Alex! Later that day Linda says good bye, until tomorrow my Hamish! She kisses him with deep abandon as she heads home.

The wedding is all planned out. Hamish is picking up is friend and they will be spending the night away from Linda on a traditional no seeing the bride the night before the wedding. Jenny comes over with Vie and Doris and her mother and they all spend the evening drinking a little and having lots of girl talk.

A little later one of the female agents from the night shift brings Fiona from the air Port and Linda says you can stay here Or Vie says or with me we have the room and Jenny says Fiona I know you prefer ladies and I am available for just fun. Linda says but first things first sense she is the ex-wife of my intended I get to kiss her first.

That kiss could melt the chrome off a Harley Motorcycle. Damn you have learned honey. Jenny is next and there embrace lasts for a long time. Come on girls break it up. It is really late and I need some sleep the big day is tomorrow. Oh and Fiona the wedding is in the nude. In the nude huh! Well I always wanted to do one like that.I will get to see what I could have had from you gorgeous ladies. You will later with me Fiona Jenny says. Linda says go get her tiger! Will do Linda!

That night Linda spent it alone in bed and dreamed of Hamish and of the kids they may have. She woke up that morning at her normal time of 5 a.m. and Jake was sleeping on her naked chest. She gets up and fixes breakfast and eats a plate of scrambled eggs and vegetables and a large glass of milk. After about an hour she puts on a pair of her very tight spandex short shorts and crop top and her Nikes and gets her badge and her pistol and her cell phone.

She steps out and goes to where she normally goes to and warms up for her usual time. Then she starts out with a jog and then speeds up. After about a mile she looks back because she has a feeling between her shoulders and sees two men running on the same trail. But it looks like they do not have running gear on. She decides to speed up a bit and see if they are trying to follow her.

Both men over compensate and sprint towards her. Linda has the knowledge of the trail and quickly races at full speed and rounds a bend and gets behind a large boulder and crouch's down and pulls her pistol. They both come around the bend with their pistols out.

They swear in French and quickly look around for their target. Linda sites in on the closest one and mentally says to herself. Damn it! I have to play by the rules. She gets her badge out and quickly steps out from behind the boulder and says freeze Federal agent, drop your weapons and then put your hands up.

The closet quickly turns and points his pistol at Linda and is about to fire when she puts a bullet through the forearm of the hand holding the pistol. He drops it from his nerveless hand and cradles his bloody arm.

The other one advances on Linda and says in a heavy French accent. I will take you down without a gun Bitch. Linda replies Talk is cheap asshole! Linda sees he is getting in a classic savate stance and she puts her gun away and gets ready and motions him to start. He advances and starts a series of kicks that snap out and back. She blocks all of these with her forearms and her legs.

Then he twists and turns in a set pattern and then gets closer and he snap kicks and he connects and she get hit on her leg hard. Hey asshole I am getting married this afternoon I do not need any bruises. Then come with us quietly and you will not be harmed. Right like I am going to go with you. As you wish then.

He launch's another kick and Linda dances out of the way and does a reverse crescent kick and catch's him across his side and he lets out a grunt of pain. Then Linda comes forward and elbows his jaw and his head snaps to the side and blood drools out of his mouth.

He stands up and does a side mule kick and it almost reach's her knee. She shifts her stance and brings her elbow down on the side of his extended knee and she hears him gasp in pain. Then she does a very American move. She swiftly kicks him in his balls. She crush's them so hard that he violently vomits up bile and breakfast as he welcomes the darkness of the unconscious.

She sees the other one trying to run away and she runs him down and has her gun out pointed at him and motions him to where the other one lies on the ground still blacked out.

Linda disarms them and calls the office and has them picked up and sent to a secure hospital. Then she finish's her run and hits the weight room. She gets her six inch wide belt on warms up again and lifts some solid weights for an hour.

She heads back to her apt. and gets cleaned up and gets in a suit for the office and goes in and fills out a report and sees Alex there. She gives him her report and he says why are you here this could wait. I know Alex but all the details were still fresh in my head and the discharge of a firearm still needs to be reported right. Yes Linda you are right! I was only going to come in and fill out the report and go home and get cleaned up and go to my wedding.

I am glad you will the one to give me away Alex it means so much to me. You are welcome Linda now go home and I will get a report to you as soon as I have it on those guys.

Linda gets up and says see you later Alex! She gets in her 4X4 and goes home. There she strips and gets in the shower again and thinks of Hamish. Afterwards she dries off and puts on talcum powder. Then she puts her best tanning oil in her handbag and puts on her best wrap around dress with nothing on underneath.

She puts on her sandals and has everything in her bag and goes to her mothers. Once there Linda sees that Scott has everything under control.

She goes to the back yard and agent Harris is there plus about the whole office staff and some of the wives are there. Nobody has taken their clothing off yet but her mother comes out still dressed and says good morning my precious daughter. They hug and kiss each other and her mother says you need to one get inside to your room and get naked.

Wait for me to say her comes the bride and you come out and Alex will walk you down and give you away. It should be in about fifteen minutes. She goes back to the bedroom and Jenny is in there and says her I will help you. Jenny I am getting undressed not putting on a wedding dress. Oh but I know you Linda. You will want to have your best tanning oil on. Yes you're right. Well I will put it in the places you cannot reach. I will also be helping out Hamish in a few minutes he is in your mother's room and No I will not grab his Willy.

Okay my friend, get him oiled up as soon as you're done with me. Jenny puts the rich tanning oil on Linda's back and Linda asks her. Am I doing the right thing by getting married? For most of my life I was a lesbian and now in just a few short weeks I have switched sides. Jenny says this. If you have to ask that question then my dear friend you are doing the right thing.

But ask yourself this. Do you love Hamish and does Hamish love you. Yes my dear friend I do love him. He has said he loves me. Well them you have answered your own question.

Thank you my dear friend. No problem Linda. Now I have to oil up your handsome husband and I promise to not grab his Willy.

Linda sits in her room all oiled up and making sure her makeup is right and hair is looking good. Then her mother knocks and enters and says well Linda I see you are ready. Yes mother you should strip to. Oh! I will here in a minute. Have you any thoughts of kids Linda" Yes mother I have and I want at least two. Well good I want grand kids to.

She unties her dress and gets out of it and has Linda put some sunscreen on her back and within a few minutes they are ready. Her mother says Hamish is all ready out there and everybody is totally naked. Well then I had better not wear my sandals huh!

She comes out and Alex is waiting on her with Vie by his side. Both have no clothing on and Vie seems to have calmed Alex down again. Linda comes forward and says! You ready boss! Yes Linda I am ready!

Vie and Linda's mother go out first and then a male and female agent from the office both naked have the rings on pillows and they walk out. Then Linda and Alex walk out and it looks like the whole office has showed up and they all have their clothing off including the wife's of their agents.

As they walk down the aisle Linda has a smile as wide as can be and she sees Hamish and her heart yearns for him. Hamish sees his love and his heart about bursts from his chest he wants her so much.

Going down the aisle Alex says those two attackers this morning were French foreign legend and there will be more. At the reception we will discuss it more but now you will be getting married. They get to the end and Alex motions for Hamish to come over and stand next to his bride.

The ceremony lasts about twenty minutes and in the end the pastor says I now pronounce you man and wife. You may kiss your bride sir. They have a kiss so passionate that it is obvious they want each other.

Linda whispers I wish we could take care of that my husband. My wife so do I. Linda's mother comes up and says you two go to the bedroom for a few minutes and take care of his problem. They run up the aisle way and go in the house. They head to her room and within a minute they are making love and taking care of his problem.

A little while later about twenty minutes has passed and both of them come out and there have a look of satisfaction and smiles on their face. They come out and mingle with all the other guests and all the guys from the office want a hug from Linda which she gives them and she gives all there wife's a hug to.

She also gives Alex a big hug and a kiss and says thank you my dear sweet friend. Vie comes up and says you muscling in on my man.

No mame I am not! Linda grabs her in a big hug and kisses her and says you are a good friend to thank you for being there for me when I needed the help. You're very welcome Vie says returning the hug and kiss.

Hamish walks over with Fiona who is still naked and Linda says you are one sexy lady Fiona. Thanks you are quite the looker to. Linda says I owe you this and I was promised I could so come here. Linda and Fiona lock lips and Hamish looks on in admiration at his present wife and his ex-first wife kissing with such passion.

They part a few minutes later and Linda says wow! You know how to kiss! Hamish says I could have told you. Our sex life was great but MI6 was the crimper on our love life. Right Fiona! You are to right Hamish. They do not mind I am a Lesbian It is just I have got every shit job ever sense I was moved to MI5.

Alex says Fiona I am working on a project and it will take the combined efforts of several operatives from several nations.

What's this Alex, Linda asks? Well Linda sense we have taken you on our little office we have had more tasks come up and our work load has gone up to. I have sent a proposal to the president to see if we can form a joint task force of multi-national agents. That will have to go before the United Nations security boards but if we do this right we can get it done within a few months and I can request anybody I like from any agency that signs on. I am sure that MI5 will sign on and I will get you two. We will get several other agencies around the world to sign on as well.

That is a great idea Alex I like that. Fiona says I would join it. It sounds like you have a good grasp on how to treat you agents. Thank you Fiona Alex replies. As requested there were no gifts other than one. Hamish's friend! The one who owned the one Island he said within the next four months not much will be happening on my island. Just let me know and the place will be stocked for a couple weeks with food and drinks. All very fresh and you will have the place all to yourself. Thank you Ted that is really good of you! Ted says the only price is that I kiss the bride!

Pucker up cowboy I will lay a kiss on you that melt the chrome off of a Harley. After their lip lock both part and Ted says paid in full wow Hamish you have a wife that can kiss. Linda says thanks you.

Linda's mother comes over and says you two love birds. Linda and Hamish stand before her mother and she says! When I got you when you were six years old! You were a cute little girl then. I decided then that I would treat you with all the respect a true daughter should have. I gave you my love and my heart. But a bad man toke some of that away.

But we survived and became even better friends afterwards. I had always hoped you would marry a guy but when you told me at that very young age that you would never have anything to do with a man ever again. I was heartbroken for you.

I was a tiny bit selfish and wanted grand kids but I figured that time heals all wounds. Well it took about twenty eight years to get over that wound. It took the right man and with a little help from the right friends.I guess what I am saying is I am happy for you Linda and

Hamish you are a good and decent man. I see it in your heart. Be kind to one another. Remember Love concurs all!

Both Linda and Hamish lean down and kiss her on her cheeks and the tears of joy flow from them. Later on after the reception has wound down and almost everybody goes home. Alex tells Hamish what happened that morning.

My word Linda how many were there. Oh Luv I handled it this time, I was out for a run and they came out of now where and followed me. They have had to be in good shape to get that close to me so fast.

You said they were the French foreign legend, they are. Then Alex gets a phone call and he answers it. After a minute he hangs up and says those guys talked under the Sodium Pentothal and they did not have a poison tooth.

They were told to grab you and rough you up and do what they wanted with you and hold you captive until they could get further instructions. It is unclear where they would get the instruction from all they said was they would be met. At a prearranged place!

We have the place and we have a couple of agents working to look like them and seeing if we can work that angle to. Great now all we have to do is see about finding those two weasels.

That Linda and now your new partner Hamish will need to work on. Hamish! Linda asks let's get to my place and have at least a nights pleasure and then go to work in the morning.

Oh Alex I do not plan on changing my work out routine just because some Terrorists want me dead. I will have an agent with me now and he will watch my back and front.

All right Linda that will be fine! But just in case I will use the treadmill I have available and do my run that way.

Chapter Ten

That night Linda and Hamish had a very intense honeymoon and a quick dinner. That next morning Linda and Hamish go the Apt. complex's workout room and they have two treadmills. Sense it was early, nobody was there they both get on and start after a good warm up. Linda has hers programmed for an uphill run at a good pace and Hamish is just jogging.

Afterwards Linda and her husband hit the weights hard for an hour. After that they head back to her Apt. and take a shower together and have a quickie and get ready. Linda dress's in a black dress pants and a backless black top with a black jacket she clips her badge to the waistband and her pistol in a belt side cross draw holster.

Hamish only has his suitcase from his assignment and puts on his black jeans and he puts and a white pull over shirt. He puts his Glock pistol in an inside the waistband holster. Both of them have three clips of ammo each.

They get to the office and Linda gets him settled at a desk near hers and gets him logged on to the network and shows him the databases and the links to the other agencies.

Doris comes in with Fiona and Jenny. Jenny says I have to be going home tonight so my dear friend I will see you again soon I have a feeling I will. I hope so. Keep in touch.

Jenny says Oh I cannot keep a secret from you any longer. She says could you get Alex in here, Vie too please. Sure! She calls them on the phone and a minute later they both come in.

Alex asks what is going on Linda? Linda replies ask Jenny she asked you come in here. All right young lady could you please tell us why you got me away from my very important paperwork. Sure this, She reaches in her back pocket and pulls out a slim wallet and hands it over to Alex. She is smiling the whole time. Alex gets an amused face and hands it back and says you might as well tell them Jenny. Linda says tell us what.

Well my dear friend after I was asked to leave the air force, that entire stink I could have raised I almost did. But the base commander did one better than the honorable discharge I could have received.

You see Linda I went to college and I had been to officer training school. I was commissioned as well. But the story of me getting let out of the military was a smoke screen. I am still in the Military. In fact I am a full colonel as you are. I am a member of the Office of Military Intelligence. I know an oxymoron by a lot of people.

Yes Linda I know I hated to deceive you and when you got this job I knew one day I could tell you. That day is today. Alex says so Jenny why are you telling us this now. Well actually I am not supposed to tell anybody I have broken just few regulations just by saying this much.

But your little speech yesterday prompted me to ask you if you have included the military in on that joint task force. Alex replies I know I did. Well if you could please put my name on the list of people to apply for a position. I would be happy to, and do you have a resume? She hands over a couple of sheets of paper and he looks it over and says I know a lot of these operations. You were on these. Yes Alex I was, in fact I was in charge of about a third of them.

Good. I will defiantly put yours and Fiona's name on my list. Now! Just to get the old man to sign off on it. Then the United Nations joint security board to sign off on it.

So as it stands now it is on his desk right now. He said that I would know today if he signs it or not. So Jenny could you give us a hand until you have to go back to Germany. Sure but I do not have to go. I have been tasked to find these very same terrorists on my own and to us what I see fit as help. I see it fit that I help up to help me. Oh Linda I was hoping that when the OSI came calling on you that you would answer those questions that I set up the right way.

You gave them the questions to ask? Yes I did. I did not want the life of a very dear friend and a very good Officer to be known as a lesbian and be booted from the Air Force. Alex said you used your office to arrange that Linda say in the service. I only arranged the questions.

If she would have answered any other way than she did I could not have helped her? But I knew Linda was smarter than that. Sneaky Alex says I like that. Linda replies for that my dear friend you have my lasting love. Hamish says what about me? Oh Luv you will always have my everlasting love.

People we have a trio of terrorists to catch. Jenny coordinate all finding with Linda she is the lead on this case in my department and for now I will see about getting you assigned here as well. I will find a way to not let them know you let on to us who you worked for. Thanks Alex! Sheesh! The things I do for those I like.

Jenny pulls up a seat next to Linda and Hamish and Fiona come over and pull up a seat and for the next three hours they brain storm many ideas and possible scenarios that may yet occur.

They send out Query's to the Pacific shipping yards in the states and Canada and Mexico. To keep a look out for these types of shipments! Also Linda Ask the Nuclear Regulatory Commission to check up on that Isotope that was found her in the states and was from the Chernobyl reactor. As the messages get sent out from her desk and her new team she is getting to know she realizes that she may only have just a few more weeks to track down the three responsible.

There's Hans and then there are the two Taliban operatives. Linda sends out the notice to see where Hans is right now. She thinks he is the key to getting the rest of the info. She sends her request off to Alex and the reply is I will find out.

Mean while Linda says it is lunch time and I am having it catered today. There will be Pizza and all kinds of different Italian meals and enough to feed this entire office. Also they have been cleared to cook and deliver to here. Lunch arrives and there is literally enough to feed a small army.

Soon everything is devoured and all that is left is the cleanup which takes all of ten minutes.

The NRC calls back an hour after lunch and says we have a problem. It appears that when we asked about that rod we got answer we did not like. It appears that about a two foot section of that rod was missing. In addition to that what was recovered by your office? So about two feet that very nasty stuff is missing.

It would make one hell of a bomb and very dirty. Yes but could it be used to irradiate really fine metal shavings and be released into the air that way and become fall out. He replies It would have to have a very powerful delivery system and something to carry it like a pesticide or something thing like that. Thank you commissioner you have been a big help. Linda seats her herself in front of her computer and composes a report that would possibly change the profile of the mission. An hour later she has saves her copy and printed up two more. One she files and the other she passes' to her team. They all drop their jaws and Linda says I have to take this to Alex ASAP.

The team as one stands and says we will go with you. She says get him a mug of coffee and get one your self's. She calls Vie and says I need to see Alex As Soon As Possible. She says I will buzz him and I will ask when. Thirty seconds later she calls back and says He is free now. Good! Thanks Vie and you need to be there as well.

They get there and Linda hands him the coffee and he asks what's this? That is coffee and this is a very disturbing report!

He reads the report and looks up at Linda's team and says you know what this means. We go to condition level two alert! That means we have to stay in constant communications with the home base and the president has to be notified and the joint chiefs. Also the other agencies will be notified as well.

Linda I hope you know that if they do that they could kill millions not just thousands. A Radioactive cloud like that could circle the whole earth before it is dispersed enough where it could cause no more harm.

I am well aware of that. I have the figures on a separate report for you if you need them. Send them to me and I will send them up. Okay but here is a hard copy. She hands him the other three pages she has in her folder.

Alex says all right get back to work and find that nerve gas or a delivery system.

Fiona says we need to call your national weather service and get weather predictions for the next thirty days and prevailing winds. They could set it off in a western city like San Francisco or someplace like that. Fiona you have access to our computers now anyways that's your task.

Hamish my husband please see about getting the Canadian borders set up with Geiger counters. We need to send out queries on the state of local health around the nation. See if there is anything matching what we went through here and anyplace around the United States. Go back about six months. If you do not find anything go back a year. Alex comes in on the tail end of this and hands Linda a form and please sign this Linda. She looks at it and picks up a pen and signs it and then hands it back to Alex and asks why me! There are a lot more agents out there who are more qualified than I am.

That may be true Linda but the president seems to think that you will do the job nicely and so do I. Now hand over your gold badge and take this Other Badge I have in this pocket. It will proclaim you the first member of my new international task force and the lead special director. And Hamish my boy you will have one s just like your dear wife's With that Badge and the I.D. you will get in a few days will get you into any country in the U.N. without the need of a passport but I would suggest keeping one on file here.

Also I will have forms for all of you soon enough to sign. Linda asks how's come this all happened so fast Alex. Well it was Jenny and Doris who sent their own reports in and you were named a lot in them both.

Thanks you two Linda says! Well Jenny says when I saw how much effort you put into finding those three and all your reports I was able to read. I knew you were on the right track. Doris replies by saying that one you have been so nice to me and helping me with my reports. I decided to do some digging myself when you were in Panama with Hamish.

All three profiles you have narrowed down the search from months to just a few short weeks.

Alex says and those last two reports I sent up to the President and the joint Chiefs erased any doubt they had about you. Not that they had any before. You and Hamish will be flown tomorrow to the president's office and sworn in as the first of the Joint U.N. Security task force with international police powers and that power is at the country level. Here in the states you will be equal to me.

Alex you can not mean that. I will always look up to you!

Thanks Linda! I like that.

But the Charter holds that you will have the authority to do what is needed and get it done.

Vie and I and Hamish will be going with you tomorrow. Hamish as your equal in command! He will soon have his own team of agents mostly MI5 and so forth.

Later that day Hamish comes up to Linda and sits next to her and well Luv I never fancied me with you as my boss. Neither did I Luv.

Think of this though you get to have wild sex with the boss and she will not sack you for not being able to keep it up. Hamish smiles and laughs and Linda laughs at the poor joke and they kiss and Linda says you need a suit for tomorrow and so do I unless the President would not mind us naked.

Somehow Luv I do not think that would be a good idea. You're right Luv! After a day of tracking down leads. Then finding a few promising ones! Linda and Hamish head out and go to a decent store that has worked with the Justice Dept. in the past for men and ladies who need a good stylish suit with a bit extra room for a vest and a hand gun.

Linda goes with a full standard Black with thin gray pinstripes and a backless top like she has now. The jacket has a Kevlar lining in it that will stop a .45 cal bullet.

Then Hamish gets a standard three piece suit that looks just like his wife's. So they match. Then they go home and make sure they are packed for a day in the nation's Capital.

That night before she goes to bed she calls her mother to ask her to look in on Jake tomorrow as she and Hamish has to go out of town for a day but will be back that night. We will leave my truck at your place. But it will be early so you do not need to be up. That's fine dear her mother replies!

That night's love is filled with passion and they both go to sleep satisfied.

That next morning they wake early and eat a quick breakfast. Linda has scrambled eggs and orange juice and Hamish has the same but he also has toast with his. They get there suits on and Linda straps on her pistol and new badge and Hamish does the same with his and they both take a small duffel bag and leave. It is still early morning and the sun is not even up yet and it promises to be a very hot day indeed.

They get in her truck and drive to her mothers and park it. On the way over Hamish calls for a ride to pick them up at Linda's mothers place and take them to the Airport.

Doris is up and outside with Scott who has been assigned to Alex's team for the moment and both seem very happy. Scott says what you're getting a very high honor Linda I am glad it is you. I only wish I can be on that team some day.

Tell you what send your agency resume to Alex and I will see it and most likely make my recommendations.

But Because I know you I will have you assigned anyways but go through the process that way nobody will pick up on the fact I assigned you without the process.

There ride gets there and they get to the airport. They go around the airport security in such a way that only they could with their permission. They see her badge and wave her and Hamish through. Five minutes later Alex and Vie show up dressed up and ready Alex have a small duffel bag with him as well. Okay people all aboard. They get on the Government Lear jet and get seated and belted in. The pilot says we should be there in about two hours max. No problem Alex says the meeting is not until this afternoon. We have to complete a few more forms for Hamish to be able to take that position as your equal in command.

You do want this job Hamish do you?

Yes Alex I do! It is a dream job for us in the community. I am glad because you seem to me like the man who can do this with his wife in charge. I am glad Alex and I would be able to help out in ways I could not before.

Linda has taught me so much in the past few weeks than I have ever learned. Oh it was not about being a spy or an agent of a government but how to help people and how to find details and others things.

Well it seemed to have helped because you will be her equal in command and can take the right actions that need to be made.

They all relax a bit until they land. Hamish even has a nap on the flight. Linda wakes him with a kiss and says wake up sleepy head were in D.C. they all unbuckle and when the Lear jet has stopped they open the door and the temperature here is about the same back home, about the same Hot!

They walk to the Black Govt. SUV and get in and ride in Air Conditioned comfort. After about forty minutes they get to the White House and they go in the Side entrance where there are all asked to get out and see their authorization and business here. Alex tells them and they are all business but very nice and polite though out the whole ordeal.

They call up and receive confirmation and they continue on their way. Alex says that is about the best security I have seen in a while and very polite.

Linda says I will be sure to pass that along when I can. They park and go inside. The secret service met them; again ask for their I.D. and Badges. Alex does not seem upset by the multiple levels of security but is for the best for security.

They are lead to an office where an agent has several forms all laid out for Hamish and the first thing he asks are you married sir. Why yes I am to Director King.

Then Director if you would be so kind as to show me the marriage license and blood test and sign on this line he will not have to get a green card and he will have dual citizenship. Linda shows him the license and blood test paperwork all properly notarized by Alex.

After all the paper work is done the agent says well from this moment on you are the Associate Director to Director King. But the Man wants a small ceremony on the Oval Office. That's cool Linda says! Well I will say this you and your husband and both Alex and Vie are allowed to carry your weapons loaded while with the president and his guest. Who is his guest Linda asks. He is somebody special and that is a surprise.

The time comes and they go up to the Oval Office and there are two Marine color guards there and they are standing ready.

Linda says looking sharp men keep it up as she produces her badge. They briskly salute and she returns the salute with equal briskness.

They go inside and the president stands up and so does the Prime Minister of United Kingdom, England! Hamish is amazed and so is Linda that they would go to this much trouble for them. She says hello Mr. President and Hello Prime Minister and shakes their hands. The president says come over everybody; sit down. There is a small set of couches and chairs off to the side with a couple of large carafes coffee. The president greets Alex and Vie like old friends and Hamish clasps the hand of his Prime Minister.

They all sit and talk a few minutes about the current case and the President says this looks grime. I will have to tell our public something. But you leave that to me and my people. I need you Director King and your new husband along with your team and Alex's team to find these terrorists and bring them to justice.

I will do my very best sir Linda says!

I know you will; now as to this little ceremony, I get to have just a tad bit of fun giving you this piece of plastic.

So after their coffee they go and stand in front the president's desk in the Oval office and he presents to her I.D. and again hands her badge to her and she shakes his hand and a picture is taken and then the Prime Minister hands Hamish his Badge and I.D. and his picture is taken.

He hands her certificates of office and says these are for you and to confirm you are now a director of this joint task force. You will still regionally report to Alex but also to the chief of staff and last but not least me the president. By the way that charter is permanent.

After some more handshakes and a few hugs the president says you will get a couple of things to jump start your operational status. One all the money that has been seized by legal means from your present operation will help you with maintaining your operation until a budget is ascertained.

Next I will let you equip your team and facility with captured hardware and a lot of that is Military grade. A location needs to be found.

Alex says I have some thoughts on that. I would suggest on or near a military base with an active runway. Linda says this all sounds fantastic when can I start? The president says after you leave here you will be taken to a couple of warehouses and the sky's the limit or actually what we have in there within reason Please!

After several more thank you's and well-done's they all leave and the marines are still just as professional as ever. Linda remarks to the president that on the way in the security was very polite and professional I would like to pass on my thanks to a job well done by them to them. The president says I will see to it personally. Thank you sir!

Leaving was a lot easier than getting in. They all got back in the Black SUV and headed out and the agent driving said security will be very tight at this compound.

That's fine sir! We will most likely be getting something from this warehouse and other one as well.

Alex I have decided to set up operations on a military base. There will be layers of security then and that is better all around. I will set up in the one south of the city. Vie says I know the one and they would welcome an increase in the Operations tempo and there Air Force so I will know the lay of the land so to speak.

They get to the first warehouse and security is a lot tighter than on the president. They finally getting inside and Linda is handed a clip board and she sees that there are all kinds of full automatic weapons.

The first thing she checks is the Mini-Uzi's.

There are couple of hundred of them. She signs for two hundred plus over four hundred clips for them. Then all available nine millimeter parabellum ammo which is about five hundred thousand rounds of ammo. With silencers for the Uzi's!

Then she sees on the list of about one hundred and fifty .45 caliber Glock pistols with 9 round magazines. There are also three hundred magazines available so those are put in the pile. She has ten Barrett light fifty sniper rifles added along with a thousand rounds over assorted ammo for them. She also gets all available holsters that are in there for the weapons they need them for.

She puts in the paperwork to have .45 Caliber ammo made available to her operation and all that is at this ware house is to be shipped to her new base of operations within the next few days. She says ok sir that should do it here I let us go to the next warehouse. After a fifteen minute travel time they get to the next warehouse and security is just as tight. They get through it with no problems and they get in and there are vehicles of all kinds in there. They have the typical Black SUV but Armored Linda says I want ten of those and there is a special one with a mini-gun that comes up out of the top and can fire about five thousand rounds of 5.56 millimeter ammo a minute. Linda says I want that to and all the ammo I can get.

There is also a fairly new armored limo in there which Linda says would want.

Then she sees a small helicopter. A four person model that is all blacked out. She asks the agent there does that operate. He replies Mame!

Everything in here was in top operating status last month. We go through every two months and do a complete operations check on everything within reason. Then add it to my list and it says you have a large stock pile of Israel body armor new and never even been worn by their troops. Well because the contractor screwed up and sent them all black not desert camo which they wanted. It is also a higher protection factor than they ordered. Great I will take it. That should do it for now.

Linda says I need to get going and set my base of operations. Alex says normally this all takes place over about a year but Linda you only have just a couple of days so you will be getting all the help you need. Plus the base you will be at does not have enough security police I am having a whole squadron sent to you and all of them are active duty with high security clearance.

Good. They leave and Linda gets on her phone and calls the people to come and get this equipment and get it moved to my new head quarters.

They head out and back to your base Alex and from there I will start my set up If that is all right.

It is Linda and I will be lending a hand getting you started.

They finally get back to the office and Linda packs up her desk and Alex says you forgot one thing Linda. What's that Alex? Computers and the security for them! I did forget a big item. Not to worry Linda I have that covered. Sense you will not have a full staff at first I can see about getting thirty hi end laptops sent to you with a sever and a T3 line installed at your location or at least a T1.

Thanks Alex that is thought full of you.

Your welcome Linda!

Linda decides to go to the base where she will be setting up her operations and once she gets there she produces her Military I.D. and asks gate security where the base commander's office is at. He points the way and salutes Linda and she returns the salute.

She pulls in and goes inside and sees the secretary. Linda says I need to see the base Commander please! Just a moment Mame she replies. She gets on the phone and calls him. She says just a moment he is on an important phone call from some real high up person. Linda smiles and says I bet I know who.

Is there anything you want to tell me Colonel King the Secretary says? That's classified. But I have clearance she says. Linda replies not this high. Sorry Mame!

A minute later a man steps out of the office and comes over and says you must be Colonel King. Thanks for seeing me on such short notice sir. Shall we go in! The information I am about to tell you is for your ears only.

They get inside and he gestures to a couple of nice arm chairs and she sits down and then he does. He says I was just on the phone with a very high up government official who says you will need a couple of buildings and two hangers on my base. Yes sir that's right. Did he tell you that you will get an increase in a couple of things and increased in operations tempo and a budget increase to help with that? Yes he did and you will be getting a whole squadron of security police in just for your areas security. That's true. But they will only be here long enough that when I am established we can them provide our own security.

One thing Colonel King I assume the rank is not a real rank. Oh no sir It is real I am a Full Colonel in the air force. But my direct commander is the chairman of the joint chiefs. But please call me Director King. I am the new head of a joint security task force for the U.N. and I have the pull to do a lot of things.

Like in the next couple of days I will have lots of equipment brought in and put in those hangers and the buildings. There will be multinational people here that will work for me and your own security squadron will increase its own staff by one hundred percent for the added security on base.

Also to point out one small thing I used to be in the air force so I know how a base should work. All right Mame! I can show you where your new office will be. That would be fine but I have to get going here in a little while. I have to get back north. I still have some terrorist to catch. Oh yea! The news and some of the security reports I get said that they had a task force looking for something along those lines. Yes I have been looking for them for some time. They get there and go inside the hangers and it looks good inside. The commander says we just had these two redone and they are in good shape.

They check out the two building and the smaller one used to be a security police building complete with armory. It is still in good shape. So Linda says this one will be my head quarters and the other one will have offices and such for all my other agents once I get to full strength.

When do you think that will come about? Colonel he asks? That is a good question sir! I do not know!

After that they go back and Linda says thanks for the tour and I will see you within the next few days with my associate director

He is also my husband and has dual citizenship with Great Britain. Oh an English man. Yes sir!

Linda leaves the base and heads back to Alex's head quarters and she goes inside and sees Vie and says I am tired Vie. I know the feeling. Travel always does that me.

Linda goes in and sees Alex and he hands her a stack of forms. He says these are transfers from this office and a couple of others. At the top of the list is Agent Harris and Linda says I do not want Harris.

He is your number two guy besides Vie. I will not leave you with out a good back up man. And he is good. He could have this office some day.

But with me he would not get that. I know that Linda I had to let him put his request in. Sorry Alex it has been a long day. The facilities down there are fine but need work. Like you said even with all this help we are not going to be at full strength for some time.

The rest of the requests she signs off and Scott and Doris are now hers permanent. She also asked can they keep their equipment they had issued to them here please! Sure thing!

Alex says that is part of the help we set up. That they keep their gear because it already fits! Linda does say I will need access now to order night BDU's for them. Alex turns his laptop around and says click on that link and order away and then enter your pass code and it will come out of that one point five million spend budget you have.

She orders an assortment of sizes of uniforms and head gear plus cold weather gear as well. Plus boots, thermal underwear, socks. She logs in her pass code and the money is transferred. She will get her shipment with the next week or so and it will go to the new head quarters. Linda says I need to get some sleep as Hamish brings in a mug of coffee for all of them. She sees he already has become more relaxed around everybody. Linda says Hamish I need you to screen the applicants tomorrow that will file in their requests. I have signed these for Alex they will transfer down tomorrow.

Now though I need a five mile hard run and hot shower with a good meal. Well Linda how does a meal over at my place sound tonight. Vie says I am cooking it and I do believe it is your favorite is fish on the grill. Yes it is! Well go home and do your run and then come dressed very casual, we will be as well. All right we will be there in a little while.

Make it about an hour and a half ok. Sure thing! Before they get inside Hamish says I have been a little busy myself. I had a tread mill installed in our apartment. Oh cool that way I can run naked! Yes you can and I can watch. Do not worry I will use it to.

They get inside and it is all set up and she quickly strips and gets her Nikes on and starts up the tread mill. Soon she has it going up a steep incline and she is running at her top speed. After which seems forever to Hamish but only twenty five minutes and five hard miles.

She kisses Hamish and says scrub my back ok husband mine. They take a quick shower and have a quickie in the shower. Then Hamish puts on a pair of shorts and a tank top with sandals. Linda goes for a white spandex crop top and a short white cotton skirt with Sandals as well.

They head over to Alex and Vies place and Linda's stomach is rumbling very loudly. Well love I am glad we will get that filled soon enough. Me to! I was not expecting to get asked out but I will make do.

They arrive and Hamish says Alex told me to just go in and yell out they would answer. Ok Linda says! They enter and it is well light up. Linda calls out and Vie answers we are out back please I want you all to make yourself at home and if you want to go naked that is fine with us. There are towels in the living room. Sure enough there are big towels there and Hamish says this was a little bit planed by me. Oh honey you are the sweetest! So Hamish says get your kit of bird!

I will get mine off as well and both Alex and Vie are naked as well. Linda is naked in less than twenty seconds and Hamish is about as fast. They both grab a towel and go out to the big fenced in back yard. Alex and Vie are there and Naked as can be. Alex he does have an apron on standing in front of a grill fixing the fish and the grilled vegetables.

Vie says welcome to our home Mr. and Mrs. O'Connell. I know you did not take his last name. Here I will call you by your married name. Vie hands her a cold beer and says you need this dear, drink up and Hamish will drive you home. Alex says you are to be congratulated on your new position it is a very good one to be in and Hamish yours is a very sweet one to be in. Both Linda and Hamish said thanks at the same time. Soon dinner is ready and Linda says I am starving Hamish says that right her belly was rumbling all the way over her.

The evening went great and they made it home by ten P.M. and Linda said I have to sleep but I am not too tired for us to still have some good sex. Nothing is better than that for sleep. That next morning Linda and Hamish get dressed in black jeans and white shirts she puts on her stiletto heels and he puts on his boots and they head in. Once there she sees that every agent is there ready to move to the new site. They all have their office stuff along with all their issued gear.

She hands them all their new badges and I.D.'s and hands the old ones over to Alex. All right agents from now on I am your new Director of operation and Hamish is my equal. If neither of us can be reached then call this office here and they will start the search. Alex is who I report to then up the chain. But I call the shots on our operations. Ok all those I.D.s I have handed you have a Military I.D. with them. You will be known as a Captain or a Major or a First Lt. They will be real I.D.'s but you are on detached service to the U.N. and it is classified. That's all you can answer. Anymore and you open up the security of our base and our integrity.

I will back you one hundred percent.

They head out and get down there in about one hour. At the gate Linda stands with the gate guard and helps him with the passes and tells everybody were to go and park.

Afterwards the first of the vehicles arrive with all of Linda's stuff she has ordered. It all goes in the hanger at first and will get sorted. Later that day the base commander is escorted in by Scott and Doris. He says you people sure work quick and your security is good. Doris says thank you sir! We do our best. Thanks sweet heart I can take care of him now.

The commander looks at Linda and says you are very personal with your people. Well this is a different type of service. Even when

I was in the military I was personal with a lot of people. I know it happens but you need to watch it. I will but what brings you here. Well we have a couple of C-130 transports wanting landing clearance and the code they gave was very high clearance. I do not have that high a clearance. Linda says let me see it. He hands over his PDA and she sees the message and she taps in a long code and the message unscrambles. Linda says the reason why you could not was it was for my eyes only. I have down loaded to my system and erased it from yours. Tell them to land and point them this direction. And please have somebody from the base transportation meet us here to help us go over the vehicles once there here.

Anything else Director King please Colonel I just want to be friends! All right I will be nice. I would hope so from a very British accented voice coming up behind him.

That is my wife you are talking to. Oh my pardon sir. Hamish extends his hand and says Freddy Wallace is my name, how is it that your wife did not take your last name sir.

That you will have to ask her and she has not even told me. And Hamish gave a wink and a smile that told volumes that he was pulling the commanders leg. Everybody had a good laugh.

The commander says oh that squadron of security police will be here tonight I have enough to get you through the night then they can take over. Good they will bunk in some Harvest eagle tents set up near our second building where they can shower and do their laundry. The chow hall will need to be able handle the additional load. I will have the moneys available when it is needed. The rest of the day the base phone people were in and they set up the phones. But Linda is having the Government phone installers in the next day to make sure there secure and to have a red phone installed a direct line to the president of the United States, and the joints chiefs, and the U.N. Security Council.

They tents get set up and they get a base housekeeping comes in and gets some rooms ready. Linda grabs one for herself if she and Hamish need some sleep. That evening the C-141 with the first two flights of security police arriving and Linda is there to greet them. She returns the salute when she shows her I.D. then she says set up in the Harvest eagle and tonight get something to eat and help the base's construction Squadron with setting up the rest of the harvest eagle tents available.

Linda talks to the Commander of the security police squadron that has come in and she is a real go getter as Linda use to say.

A Major Tammy O'Bannon, she gets what is Linda needs and walks a perimeter with Linda. Linda spots two people walking in the dark close together. She quietly comes up behind them and Grabs them both by the shoulder. She bears down and both go to the ground. Linda says to the Major I have this go back and tell them we will need a fence set up on my authority and if they give you any lip tell me.

The Major leaves and does not get a look at the two young ladies that Linda is holding down. She says ok girls please stand up. They stand and both look really scared witless.

She looks at them and sees the signs they have been kissing and just about having a lesbian affair. Linda says ok I know the regulations on this so please believe me. I do not want you in trouble. The blonde looks at Linda and says you are that new commander that is real secretive huh? Yes I am! Now please answer the question. Are you two having a Lesbian affair? Like I said I know the policy. Do not ask and do not tell. Well I am asking!

The brunette says yes mame! I started it. The blonde says you just ruined our careers. Linda says no she did not. I was a full member of the Air Force for twenty years and I am semi-retired.

I now still do Govt. work and just leave it at that.

I had a couple of affairs with a member of the same sex. But I will lie through the teeth and deny anything if you bring it up and I will report you. Now give me your names and duty phone numbers. I will be calling you tomorrow for you to be assigned to my command for a little while. I want you to have a talk with a friend of mine, she will understand. Now let's walk back before my husband gets worried.

Later that evening after Linda and Hamish get home Linda says I think we need to move closer to the base. I was thinking of getting a bigger apartment anyways.

The next day fifteen other agents arrive and they are given assignments. Linda has also packed a small suitcase with workout cloths and about noon that day she asks any agent who is there and the Major who looks really fit to work out with her on a run. The Major and Hamish are the only ones who say they can keep up to five miles. Linda knows Hamish can do Five miles. She pulls him aside and says I want to see how she performs and you get to look at my backside I know you like that. Yes Luv I do.

Linda says I have to warm up sense my age says I need to. She has on a crop top with the aim high symbol and Spandex shorts and her Nikes. The Major puts on loose shorts and a large t-shirt and Black Nikes. Hamish has his usual of loose shorts and sleeveless shirt and his old jogging shoes.

Linda starts out with an easy pace and she says I am going to speed up; my husband who is not as fast as I am will stay back with you if you cannot keep up. I pride myself on going as fast as I can. Linda does speed up and the Major speeds up with her and keep up with Linda for the rest of the way. At the end when they are all three walking because Hamish was not too far behind. The Major says you are fast that took everything I had. I will be sore tomorrow.

Well see you at chow time. After they clean up in the little room they have they are back in the nice cloths with badges and pistols exposed. Linda calls the two girls up and says who are your supervisors and your commanders so I can get you on temporary duty here. Both work in base Finance so Linda has a good reason to want them. They will help with her budget. There background is looked into really deep and they come up clean. Jenny takes over for them and she has a long talk with them.

The base is really taking shape and Linda is pleased. But we need to get going on those three terrorists. All her agents are trying to crack it. But so far no leads!

Then Hamish is going though some of his database stuff with Linda's and spots a sign! He has ten other agents check his findings and he says gang saddle up I will tell Linda we have a place to start and we just might get lucky! He says Luv we have a place here we could get two of them if we move quickly enough. Where at Luv Linda replies!

Denver. Linda say that makes sense with the high altitude there it is a good place to do that. She says let's get loaded up. Hamish says already on it.

We still have that C-141 here? Yes Luv tell them we are taking every agent with us on that transport. Everybody gets an Uzi and there issue weapon. Plus all the tasers we have and ten auto injectors with a heavy sedative in it.

We take our three heavy SUV's and the High Fire Power one. The one with the Mini-Gun!

Chapter Eleven

They all race to the hanger and get ready. Linda has contacted the Command operation on base and gave her authorization for the C-141 to be fueled for a High Priority flight to Denver. They will have three vehicles and twenty eight armed personnel on board.

Ten minutes later the clearance goes through and in-flight refueling is arranged.

Linda has her colt .45 pistol as a backup with two extended clips and the new Glock .45 is on her side with 3 extra clips. The Taser with two extra charges is on her left thigh holster and she has the Mini-Uzi with 4 extra clips and a silencer. She and everybody else has on the body armor as well. Linda did not even bother with changing into the Black BDU's she just left her Suit on and removed the jacket and put the vest on. She slipped off her shoes and slipped on a pair of Neoprene Diving slippers and has a tanto knife strapped to her right leg.

Hamish has all his stuff in a bag and will put it on while in route. A lot of the other agents have done the same thing.

Within fifteen minutes of Hamish finding the information they are on the runway loading up and the load master is getting the three SUV'S tied down with the agents help. She gets on board and shows her badge and tells the aircraft commander to get his crew armed.

He replies by whose authorization? Mine and the presidents she takes out her Badge and he says yes mame! Thank you sir Linda replies. Tell the tower when you're ready for takeoff please. But please make it ASAP. We have a couple of terrorist to capture on U.S. soil. Yes mame! He replies with enjoyment. The tower says we have to wait for fifteen minute Director King the Pilot says. Let me on the radio sir. She puts on the headset and asks for the senior controller. He replies. She gives him a coded phrase. Red Dawn destruction countdown! The Controller says give just a second to check. Roger Control Linda replies. About thirty seconds later he comes back on and says you are cleared for takeoff. The pilot replies Roger tower. Flight LK001 taking on runway three left. Coming into position now! Tower says you are cleared for fast takeoff. Roger Tower and the pilot pulls the throttle to maximum and the big jet picks up speed down the runway and takes off with still more than half the runway to go.

Linda says here is the radio frequency for the tanker and gas up there. And make with all due haste to Denver. We will be ready to disembark when you land. Keep the jet hot and we will be back as soon as possible.

Linda goes back and there are over twenty agents getting dressed into Black BDU's. Hamish is finishing with his kit and Linda helps him with his body armor and she gets hers body armor on and Hamish helps her with it.

When the agents have dressed and are somewhat settled Linda says ok lets brief on the objective. Hamish says the leads I produced are from a FBI agent who saw Hans and one of the two Taliban at a strip club. Linda says that fits Hans MO. That where I first saw him. You all should have read the mission profile by now. Everybody answers yes. Linda says Hamish the floor is yours. Hamish stands and says both were spotted about an hour ago in the club. The local feds have been notified and are surrounding the area to make sure they do not get away. They are assisting us in this and will get equal credit on the arrest. We go in and first try to taser both of them then shot them with the sedative.

If that does not track then we shoot.

Benson you have the sniper rifle right? Yes Mame he replies. Ok one other important thing. The Taliban agent will have the poison tooth but we do not know if Hans will but take no chances.

They land at a Air Force reserve base and they quickly disembark in the vehicles and Linda calls the FBI and asks for an update. They reply both are still there. Good we are on the ground and at the air reserve base leaving in a few minutes. We will be on route and you can reach us at this number.

All right Director King. She closes the connection and tells the drivers to hot foot it.

Linda then calls the local police Dept. and informs them that a situation has come up and four big Black SUV's need and escort through town to this address from the air force base. We need it now we are rolling as we speak. Sorry for the short notice but we have the area cordoned off by the FBI and we needed secrecy on this. We will get units to hold the intersections open for you Thank you sir Linda replies.

They get to the first intersection and they hit their own lights and go through.

The next one the cops are there and they keep their lights on and continue on to where the terrorists are at. Three blocks away the kill the sirens and lights. They pull over and quickly get out.

They meet up with a FBI man waiting on them and find out anymore news. They are both still in there. She asks you have a sniper up on a roof top? Yes I have one. Where, I want to put another one up. The FBI man says you are not taking any chances huh! Nope. They mean to use deadly nerve agent and send a cloud o radioactive waste into the atmosphere and kill over a million people or more. So yes I want them stopped.

Linda tells her sniper to take another building away from their sniper so as to get a cross fire. The word to open fire is Crosswalk. Ok Linda he says. All right U.N. Justice Team we move in tasers first. They move towards the strip club she sends a team of ten to the back to watch the back door and sense this is a two story structure she asks the FBI to watch that and get anybody who might be running from there.

You have a description of all three so they are considered armed and extremely dangerous. They get to the front door and Hamish says to Scott Get the bouncer out here quietly. All right and Doris has on her ball cap and really dark shades and they quickly go in and come back out a few seconds later.

The bouncer is a normal looking guy. He says what is the meaning of this? Linda produces her badge and I.D. and says we are not here to raid you. We are here to arrest two known terrorists. Terrorists he says out loud! One more outburst like that and I will put you under for a week you read me mister. Yes mame he says. She takes out three pictures One of Hans and the other two of Taliban operatives.

He points to the one with Hans and says he is inside now. Then he points to the one on the left and says this one is in there to. All right where are they sitting, away from the stages? Yes they are to the far right back corner. Where are the dancer's dressing rooms and do you have a kitchen or an office inside.

The Dancer's dressing room is connected to the stage and has a side entrance on the inside. Linda points to Scott and Doris you two take that. She points to four other agents and tells them to advance on the stage and do not worry about the dancer's they will get out of the way. She tells the other agents to sweep in and if you see Hans or this guy Taser him and then quickly shot the sedative in him.

She informs the FBI we are going in ten seconds be ready Please. We are hot he replies.

Linda goes in first and there are two fully naked dancers on the stage and they are not even that good looking.

She continues to move in with her taser held at the ready. She sweeps back and forth and Hamish spots him and taps her on the shoulder and says there he is. She advances towards him and by now the crowd inside has stopped talking and a dancer screams because she sees all this hardware and armored people in black.

Hans looks up as sees Linda and the rest of the team and speaks in German to his contact and Linda hears part of it. He says we have been found out, But I will deliver!

Linda takes a chance and snap fires at Hans but he is fast and pulls the waitress in front of the taser electrodes and she goes unconscious for the count, but he still holds her up as a shield.

Linda yells do not hit the waitress again. Hamish at the same time has his taser out and fires on the Taliban member and he hits him square in the chest and he clutch's at the electrodes and Hamish sends another charge into him and he goes under.

Then another Agent quickly pushes the auto injector into his upper arm and sends the terrorist into the dark abyss for several hours.

Mean while Hans still has the passed out waitress up as a shield and says well Toni how nice to see you again and you have on your clothing in here. What is this I thought you was a stripper and my play toy.

No Hans I am an international agent and I am here to stop you. So you are Linda King. I must say you are a very pretty lady and good in bed.

But how did you track me down? Linda replies I will let you figure that one out for yourself. But in the mean time I want you to put the young lady down and give yourself up. We will consider that a positive step towards the sentencing. Oh no! I will not go to a jail Linda King!

I would rather see the chemicals sold and make millions and live on a deserted island than that!

He keeps backing up to an unknown door they did not see when they went in. He then opens it and quickly throws the waitress to the floor and goes through the door and shuts it. Linda yells! After him!

She sprints for the door and has put her taser away and has the Uzi out. She throws open the door and gun fire goes down the stairwell and one come close to Linda. She takes a chance and quickly looks around the door and up the stairs and sees he is about to fire again. She lets a burst go with her Uzi! He ducks out of the way but he grunts in pain as one bullet tags him in the arm.

He runs to a window which he had planned to use just in case this would happen. He opens it up with ease and climbs out. He leaps down on to the top of the dumpster and then on to alley way. Linda gets a report that a man has jumped out of the window and is running away. She gets on her radio and says to her sniper can you tag him.

No way Linda! I do not see him from my angle! The other one says I do not ether.

Then as Linda and her team runs up the stairs she hears gun shots from outside. Scott come in and says he winged Doris and then he shot a civilian on a motor cycle and took off like a bat out of hell.

Linda gets on her radio and asks the FBI man I thought you said we had this area blocked off. We did. But my men are not accustomed to these situations. Fuming from the incompetence Linda closes the connection and turns over to their frequency and says how is Doris? She will be fine. Scott you did fine we always watch each other backs and never leave a wounded agent.

Outside they are getting the one Taliban operative loaded up in there SUV and Linda talks to the clubs manager. Sorry about coming in here like that but we needed to capture those two. Your waitress should be fine I will see to it the bill is picked up by my department.

He replies well at least it was just in the afternoon crowd. We will have this place fixed back up and good as new. This place kind of reminds of the places where I used to bust the young airman coming out of clubs like this. At my first base they were not supposed to be going in this one club. It was a know drug den.

Again thanks for the help. They all load up and on the way back the local have the intersections blocked off for them. Linda has Alex on the Line and tells him the news. Both good and the bad! Well I know the FBI agent there that is in charge and who you just told me was not him. Alex I think we have found some of their people! We need to move on that fast. I will get on it Linda good work I will send a certified Doctor who I trust to help with the interrogation. All right Alex Plus he did have a poison tooth and it was removed. We will keep him sedated until your Doctor arrives. ETA about four hours! I will meet you then Director King and give my regards to your team they did an outstanding job.

Even Doris for catching that stray bullet! You can tell her yourself when we land

She is coming back with us. Her boyfriend is taking care of her.

Soon they land back at the base and they drive off. Linda thanks the pilots for such a good job and gets there names, ranks and squadron they belong to and commander.

Alex greets them and sees that Doris is fine and the Doctor that came with him will look at that now. He has to wait for the prisoner is awake before he can do anything.

So he gently removes the bullet. She does not cry out just grips Scotts hand really hard. He gives her a local and puts in a five stitches and says to not go stopping any more bullets for a week.

Yes sir. Linda says take her to the room next to mine she is to get some rest and then you come back in a few hours. I need everybody's report. Get Doris's and I will help you finish it.

Later Jenny comes back and says you did well today you got one bastard now to get the information out of him. Yea but he is going to be a tough one to crack. How are those two young ladies working? They are fantastic with numbers and they are actually roommates in their dorm like we were. So you think this may grow out or do you think they will want to continue this. That is hard to say.

Linda says I will talk to them in a few days and see what else they have been thinking about.

Alex comes to her office about seven P.M. and brings her a strong cup of coffee and he says take a minute or two ok. Linda leans back in her chair and sips the strong black brew and smiles again. Thanks Alex you know just what I needed. Well Vie sends her best and Harris says hi.

That auto injector idea is a good one but we need a better sedative in it. My Doctor will be looking in on that. We need to perfect it.

Linda says here is my report I have already sent it to your computer at your office but if you want you can look it over now. He leafs though it and he pauses and reads a little deeper into it and continues and says just like I would expect for you. A very clear and concise report!

Thanks Alex!

Linda asks have you thought about which team to go pick up those double agents in Denver. Yes and I need Scott as a liaison with a team of CIA to take them in. We are going to try to taser them and knock them out but we may lose a few.

I hope not, there will be too much death already. Yes there has been! So let's keep it down Linda find Hans and let's wrap this up. I am doing the best I can. I know Linda It has been hard setting this up and your team still found them.

Thank my husband he found that bit of information that was needed. He used his credit card at this strip joint and the waitress ran it through the credit check and the system I had set up a while back sent up a red flag and he caught it.

Alex says I have to get back but call the man and let him know what is going on he will want to know. After that get something to eat and some rest the next few weeks will be trying.

After Alex leaves she and Hamish go to the officer's mess on base and Linda gets a double sirloin steak and a salad and steamed vegetables. Hamish sees they have a Sheppard's pie so he try's that and he gets a shrimp cocktail to. After that they head back to their little room and Linda slips in and crawls in between the sheets and is fast asleep in less than twenty seconds. Hamish says to himself well when she wakes she will want sex so he gets in with her naked as well and goes to sleep.

That next morning Linda wakes up and she finds Hamish in bed with her and he is looking at her. He says did you know that you have a very peaceful look when you sleep. Jenny has told her that a few times but that was years ago. Linda looks at her husband and says I am sorry I was so tired last night I just want sleep. Now I want sex and a shower and food and in that order.

For the next twenty minutes they both keep it quiet and have some of the best sex they have had in a while. Afterwards they scrub each other's back and they get dressed in clean black BDU's and strap on their equipment like a badge and from now on a vest and at least the clock pistol and steel toe boots.

They head out and stop by the mess tent for the Security police and Linda asks just for two cheese omelets and gets a tall glass of milk and two small glasses of orange juice.

Hamish gets a stack of pancakes and Bacon and sausage and milk. Hey Luv I still love this stuff and it is hard to give up. I know Luv now let's go sit with the Major.

They have small talk with the Major and when the meal is over with they are drinking some coffee a man in uniform steps in and say's room attention. Everybody in there but Linda and Hamish jump to attention!

They look and see who is coming in and steps the chairman of the joint chiefs. Linda shoots to attention very fast. Hamish does his best. The man smiles and comes over and says Sorry to drop in on like this but I was flying through and asked to stop in.

Sure thing sir! Hello again Major O'Bannon Hello sir! How do you like this assignment?

It is pleasure to work with such a delightful person as the Director here.

Thanks Toni!

Sir if you would come this way I can show you what we have so far. Sure just point the way.

They leave and go to the main hanger and go inside. There a security policeman looks at I.D.'s and crisply salutes both Linda and the four star general. He looks at the equipment they have and it is all lined up neat and tidy. The set up area is all neat and there are several agents there who are looking though the database for more clues.

The general says I do not want to disturb them, we need this menace caught.

Yes sir! I can show you one we did catch yesterday. They get to a highly secure area with no less than six Security Policeman standing around the twelve foot by twelve foot cage. The prisoner has an I.V. in his arm and he is chained to the cage itself at the ankle.

The General asks it that all necessary Director King? Yes sir it is. Doctor would you be so kind to say why to the General. Hello again General good to see you are back up. Thanks to you. OK you do not have to convince me now that I know this Doctor is on the job. But I will anyways.

He is refusing any food which will make my job when it comes to the truth serum we are going to use a little tricky. That's why I have him on an I.V. for now. As for the chain he is a bit violent. Linda adds if he gets more violent he gets strapped down and a bed pan. Which I am sorry to say we all will not like!

The General says okay Linda carry on and keep me updated! Yes Sir replies Linda. The general and his aid go from the hanger and Linda says that was an unexpected surprise. All right Doctor we will be needing results fast. When can you work on him? Within the next twelve to twenty four hours.

A few hours later a member of Linda's cyber team comes over and says Director King! I believe I have found a money trail.

Where does it lead to? The young tech answers saying the Hollywood hills and from the looks of the money spent they have been there some time.

Chapter Twelve

Hollywood! Do you have an address? Yes Mame we do! The agent prints all the information and gets it to Linda in three minutes.

Well people let's get cracking. Linda gets on the red phone and dials the Joint chiefs and says I need a C-141 Star lifter to LA ASAP. We have an address for them in Hollywood. Linda hangs up and says mount up and get your gear people we are going to the Hollywood hills and to take down a Terrorist and this time they do not get away, Right!

Everybody replies! Right! They all start to scramble and Linda puts a quick call in to Alex and tells him the situation. He says I have an Idea that will help us capture the mole as well. But leave that to me. Yes sir! Now get cracking.

The order comes in and the C-141 at the base is hot and loaded with fuel and the SUV's are loaded within the hour. All agents are loaded or loading on right now. Jenny is going and Fiona Both are leaders on their team.

They will have the SUV with the Mini gun and ten agents on their team Linda will be in overall control and Hamish will coordinate with the locals to block off the area and not alarm anybody. They land at a Marine corps base near Los Angles and disembark. Linda is on the phone talking to the chief of police and he says what is the meaning of this, and by who's authority. She replies barely keeping her rage under control. She replies The president has given me the right to do this. I

187

only contacted you because it was the polite thing to do. I will give you a coded phrase and listen well.

All police chiefs know this code. (Red Sky Blue Sky White Sky Peace).

Authentication code Tango Alpha Zeta

Authenticate reply.

Reply Authenticate Code White Blue Red Peace.

Authenticate Replied Thanks Chief you now know who you are dealing with. Yes all will be done just please keep the collateral damage to a minimum. We will do our best chief.

She hangs up and says I did not want to use that code unless Had to but he did not leave me a chose other than calling the man and that is not an option. I will not go running to him every-time somebody complains. You did the right thing Luv. Yea But I hate to throw my weight around like that.

They head out to the Hollywood hills and get within two miles of the address and the Computer man pulls up a satellite shot of the address and it shows there are lots of people there and several large buildings. Large enough to hold a couple semi-tractors and trailers inside them. Hamish says if those Lorries are loaded with that gas we could be in a world of hurt. Well I am glad we have Chem. gear along. She gets on the teams headsets and radios and sends the message for full chem. gear MOP level four.

Linda wastes little time and has the communication man contact Alex and update him. Them have him warn the President and the joint chiefs. I will call the local police.

Linda has everything on but the gas mask and she gets on the phone and calls the police chief, She says Hello chief it is me again. Your somewhat least favorite Fed.

No Director King You are not.

I received a phone call a little while ago to help you in any way I can.

Well then hold to your socks.

Those people up there are heavily suspected to have a very deadly and virulent form of VX nerve gas. Your shitting me Director king!

No I am not now my comm. guy will contact you at the first sign of any break out of chemical and will help with anything that may be needed. OK Director will do. Thanks for the heads up!

Ok! Let's roll. Mini gun deploy and taser first but if the need comes up defend and secure the place, Fire will destroy the chemical But fire will spread Radiation. So we need to watch it. Roll out.

With the precision of a military operation they roll out and sure enough there is a big Iron gate and it has two men there wearing dark Pants and a heavy coats even in the heat of LA. The gate is shut and Linda says ram it. The lead vehicle is equipped to handle that. It plows through the gate and the two men there start to go for their weapons inside their coats the driver of the lead SUV leaps out and yells Federal agent throw down your weapons or we will be forced to open fire.

As soon as he said that the one on the left draws and points an automatic pistol and starts to fire but before he can do that the agent open fires with his Glock hitting him center mass. The one on the right gingerly holds his weapon with two fingers and places it on the ground and place his hands behind his head. The agent uses plastic cuffs and he is put aside for later interrogation. Then the rest of the vehicles head up to the large house. Linda's ear piece comes on; The voice is Alex and says I have a marine detachment coming up to help you. Thanks Alex she replies Full Chem. gear Ok Mop level four. Will do Linda Alex out.

They get up to the house and start to see more guards all look to be Europe in looks. Mercenary's most likely she calls out to the

Radios and says OK people stay frosty we have mercenary's here and they know how to fight.

The all get into position with Linda, Jenny, Hamish and Fiona all leading a team. They all fine a different spot to take them on. Fiona is inside Hamish is outside on Mop up and outer perimeter and Jenny has the east side of the house and I have the west side.

Hamish will also take out the large buildings that may hold the tankers. His team sets out and within five minutes he spots five large tanker vehicles with large hoses. He says ok mates let's just take out the tires on those rigs.

They all take careful aim and fire at the about the same time. At least all the front tires went flat and a lot of the rear tires were deflating as well. Then Hamish notices and sound coming from a belt. The radiation count was climbing up fast. He say Mates get your masks on and retreat we have trouble. As they move back a Large Van breaks through the doors of a barn like building and the Geiger counter is screaming Loudly that there is dangerous radiation in that truck. He says take it down men. And he aims at the driver and they open up on it. Both front tires blow out and the driver's side widows shatters as Hamish plows a .45 man stopper through the neck of the driver. The vehicle goes about 100 more feet and shuts down. Hamish gets on the radio and says we need a radiation HAZMAT team out here ASAP.

Linda replies you ok Luv?

Yea but we are pulling back and all of us are popping our Atropine. Ok Luv fall back and mop up and take care! Jenny, Fiona Go on my mark. Mark!

Linda's team heads out and starts to taser and take out Mercenary's with some difficulty. But they are doing the job. They are agent's not combat veterans! They finally get to the end of one side and they have captured about fifty percent. The others made a different choice. They get to the end and Linda calls secure and set up a line of defense. Jenny calls her side secure and about the same gave up. Fiona says I have all in here with a big room with computers all secure. Then Linda says then where is the Bad guy at. Hamish comes on the line well Luv there is one barn in back that needs checked. Ok Luv how you all feeling.

Were good now but we will need looked at soon That atropine is giving me some nasty tastes in my mouth. I am not kissing you until you feel better. Jenny says I am free and Fiona says I will come to Take care Hamish. Right Fiona I will Watch my Bird's back Eh! Like I used to watch yours! Hamish laughs and cuts the connection and Linda says meet up by the south entrance to the house. Roger. Five minutes later they meet up and check the area for radiation. It seems the one truck for now had it in it.

They do a bounding over watch to the building out back. It is about four hundred meters away and Linda drinks deeply from her camel pack water supply as does Jenny and Fiona.

Linda whispers I hope one of our boys is inside because I will be pissed if he is not.

They get set up and Linda pulls out a little gas detector and quietly pumps it a few times with a hose pointed near the entrance. The light show green and she smiles and whispers so far no chemicals.

They get there Mini-Uzi's ready and Linda tried the door latch with great care. It turns and she holds up three fingers and mouths on three. The counts down with a slash of her finger three times and on the third time she and Jenny and Fiona Go rushing in through the door. They get in and they see three people.

One is the one Taliban leader Linda has been hunting this whole time. She plants a bullet in a knee cap and the other two go down after they have be relieved of their lives. Linda looks the place over and see's a sort of command center and a computer. She gets on her link and calls Out to the others We are secure back here bring a medical team for our one prisoner and bring the computer geek back here.

191

Then a call on her link comes in and it is from the front gate. The agent left there to guard the prisoner and tell the marines what's going on. The prisoner is looking at Linda and says I know you American slut. I have seen you dancing naked in a club of sorts. Yes you have Akakeen you have. Yes I know your name! But what you do not know Is I am a director of a joint task force chartered by the U.S. Government. It was formed just to take down terrorists like you.

With that said Linda fires her Taser at him and then pumps him full of the sedative so that they can get more information out of him. She also gingerly removes the poison tooth and secure's it.

The med techs show up and carry him off and the Marine commander comes in and says we have the perimeter secured Director. Good sir thanks!

Her hacker comes in and says I will have that system up and getting your information in a few minutes. All right Gary there are others in the house. I have those all tagged Linda and some Marines taking them and loading them up. Good work.

He gets in and dodges a logic bomb and transfers all the data to a portable Hard drive and says I can get this all decoded back at base. Should only take a couple of hours. Looks like they tried for something difficult but the Logic bomb was an easy one to shut down and get rid of.

Linda hears her name over the link again and the voice says they are from the Los Angeles Fire department HAZMAT team. What do you have up here? Linda replies! I hope you guys can handle Radiation? Yes Mame we can came the reply. All right Come on up and be careful we have the area sealed off.

Linda asks the Marine commander there would you please call your base and have several medical personnel sent up here to take care of some wounds and some possible radiation poisoning.

Will do Mame he replies.

About two hours later when all the computers are loaded up and all the nerve agent has been accounted for and she has seen a report from the HAZMAT team that there is about two feet of a very radioactive Isotope rod in that vehicle. The vehicle has to be destroyed because of the nature of the Radiation It cannot be just scrubbed It was exposed long enough to become impregnated with radiation. She and the rest of her team has finally gotten out of those hot Chem. warfare suits and the med techs have arrived and said that the Atropine was the right decision to use because even though you were not exposed all the long, But the lethality of the radiation was so much that it was necessary.

Hamish says well luv in a day we can kiss again. That would be nice Luv because I am missing you already. Linda smiles back and says I miss you to Luv. Well lets saddle up and the good Major there can take over and get this place taken care of.

She calls Alex and says we got the last Taliban guy and he did not even try to poison himself but I removed from him anyways. We had no causality's on our side but over fifty percent of the mercenary's they had here did not want to come along quietly. The others are being helped for the time being at the Marine base we landed in.

We also got the Radiation Rod and the LA HAZMAT team is handling that but the NRC needs to be called and told so we can get rid of it and some other things here.

Alex says good job Linda all that remains is getting Han's and we have him. He is in Germany right now and he does not know that the operation he helped start has been shutdown.

So Linda again good job But I know you! You want to go get him and take him alive if you can he needs to stand trial for what he has done. Oh do not worry on that I will have only a few of us go. It will be me and My beloved husband and Jenny and Fiona.

We will need a jet and clearance to get there and very fast. I do not want to lose this chance. Oh you will not we have asked the local Police to just stay back and our team will handle it.

Chapter Thirteen

They get to the airport and find a sleek New Lear jet hot and idling there with two company men at the controls. They produce ID and they are Justice dept with the Clearance needed for this. Linda says thanks gentleman I am Director King and shows her ID and Badge. They said thank you Mame!

They all climb on board and the main pilot calls the tower and says a coded phase and says buckle up we have clearance and the taxi real fast to the closet runway and with a full throttle they take off really fast. A few minutes later he calls back and says Director King there are some fresh fruit and hot coffee and some cold cuts on a platter with cheese and crackers back there. Should be enough for the trip there.

After we get to our cruising altitude of thirty thousand feet we will get the speed cranked up and refuel over the eastern seaboard and then head to Germany.

The flight should only take about fifteen hours max and I understand you target is not going anywhere. We hope so but that is what we were told. Well I also have justice dept. Issue black Skin tight suits and I see you have on the Neoprene diving boots. Those are nice to wear. Yes they are so we have a lot of things you all may need to get cleaned up and I would suggest sleep.

My feelings right now but I need to make a phone call. He reaches over and pulls out a slim cable and says this should connect with your satellite cell. She hooks up and calls Alex and tells him the situation and they will be getting to Germany about the time Hans will be out partying. That sounds good. You guys take it easy up there and remember Linda alive.

The president wants him alive and able to stand trial. I will do that Alex do not fear. Besides Even though I will want to punch his ticket he has not killed as far as I know. Oh he has Linda but he is not a regular killer. So Have your team ready to use those Tasers we got for you and the Drug sedative. She says later Alex we will be careful and bring him back alive. Alex Out.

Linda gets up and gets a black skin suit and then gets the wipes that the other agents brought with them and gets somewhat cleaned up and pulls off her Neoprene boots and then her BDU's and Hamish says uh Luv what are you doing. The pilots can see you. So what! You are my man and I am a Nudist so I do not care if they get an eye full.

She then finishes up using the whips and has Hamish wipe down her back and she dries off with a small towel and puts the Black skin tight suits on and says I like these they let me move with ease and they breath. Hamish says but you can see my bits with that thing. Well Dear Luv in a very British accent. Linda says I like seeing you bits all the time. Ok Luv I will put them on but help me get cleaned up as well. Jenny helps Fiona and Fiona helps Jenny with the cleaning and soon they were all wearing the skin tight cloths and even Hamish said It did feel good.

They broke out the food and eat enough to get filled and Linda says I am getting some sleep I am really tried. Fiona says I am still wired from the fire fight I will do a first watch and tidy up here.

Linda and Hamish cuddle together and Jenny curls up next to Fiona and goes to sleep. Several hours later Linda wakes up and the pilots are announcing that they will be mid-air refueling in five minutes. Hamish says I did not know a Lear could do that. Neither did I Luv. Jenny says They have had it for a few years now. Only the top brass get them or in case us we would for a critical mission.

Hamish pulls up a diagram of the area were Hans is supposed to be at and the night club he most likely will go to. From what everybody says he still party's like there is no tomorrow so That leaves me to believe that he knows we are coming for him. That my husband is a very distinctive possibility!

Fiona finally falls asleep and when they had landed, she has woken up and they had all eaten a second time along with the pilots. There is a black SUV waiting for them and they get taken to the base commander's office. Once inside Linda tells him that they will be conducting a live capture of a know terrorist and seller of chemical warfare weapons. We need him alive.

So Colonel King what can My office do to help out. Use your contacts with in the local police to help us in sealing to area off. That should be good enough, we have agents of another agency backing us up but they want to go get him now.

I do not blame them but we need to do this by the numbers and be smart. The mark is a sly one and has slipped through our grasp a few times already. I will ask the local Police commander to help out he owes me a big favor and I will call this in. Besides I see you have a member of my former staff with you and two British nationals with you as well. You did not think I would not remember you Jenny? Yes sir I knew you would. Linda this is the Man that helped with my supposed big stink. Oh! You are that person Linda says!

Well thanks for looking out for my good friend. And as for the two British nationals they are on my staff and the man is also my much loved husband and Co-Director of the joint task force under the Justice dept.

The Colonel asks how is Alex doing these days Colonel King. He is fine you should call him. He would like that.

Well we need to get going to round us up a terrorist and you will want to get home sometime this evening. Good hunting the Colonel says! Thanks Take care The quartet says.

They all leave and take the Black SUV with Jenny driving sense she knows the rules of the road the best. Everybody could drive them but Jenny was the best. They all strap on their hardware. Mini-Uzi and eight magazines of 9 MM Parabellum ammo.

Then Linda straps on a twelve inch long Tanto fighting knife and a pair of hard weave and high impact plastic forearm covers. Her .45 caliber Glock is in its place with 3 extra magazines. Everybody else gears up in silence as well. Hamish lays a hand on his brides shoulder and says Luv I want you back in one piece please. You will love.

I did a lot of training with knives from the Military and my sensei. But this guy from all I have read is a natural fighter. He may have some drinks in him but I have seen the man drink and he can put it away and stay straight.

So all of you stay frosty and if the chance comes up I will fight him and take him alive. But all three of you watch and if he looks like he is going to take the upper hand taser him a couple of times. His constitution should be able to handle it.

They get to the first of where Agents are waiting on them. They all produce I.D. And report that he is indeed in the club at the address just up the street.

They park the SUV and get out and make their way up the street. Once there Linda asks for one of the nicer dressed agents to go in and find out where he is and get the club manager out here. Will do.

He speaks in to a small microphone and a young lady comes out a minute later with a tall medium build man. Linda asks in German are you the Club Manager? Yes and who are you. I am with the Justice department of the U.S. And also I have the authority of Interpol on terrorist activities and we know there is one.

A Han's Greuber, But we need your cooperation in this so that nobody gets hurt. The female agent tells the club manager we found his date last night! She was close to death and had been brutally raped and the over dosed on a date rape drug. He replies I had no idea, How is the young lady now.

She will recover but the emotional scaring is permanent. Linda is seeing red now. How's come I was not told of this Young lady? We just found out about fifteen minutes ago our self's. She is being taken care at the bases hospital She is a member of the U.S. Air force. Linda says I want her to have the best care and I need her name. She and a few other will have to stand up in court to testify against him on that alone.

The agent gives Linda the name and She calls Alex and gives him to current situation and to also have that young lady reassigned to her command back in the states as soon as possible. Alex says you ok Linda?

Yes sir but I wish I could just take him down. Hamish and my other friends with me said that they will taser him if it get out of control. Ok sounds good let me know the outcome Alex out.

Okay we are going in. They all head inside and the Manager gives a signal to the doorman to send word to the waitress's and waiter's that the police are here to take a person into custody. Linda looks inside out on the dance floor and see's Han's having a good time with two young ladies at the same time. Linda says let's try and get him surrounded. The waiter's have cleared some of the people out of the way buy telling them there is a dance contest in the street and that's makes it a lot easier for the four to quickly move in and surround Hans.

As soon as they get around him the two other CIA agents pull the girls to safety and the DJ kills the music.

So Ms King of the Justice Department you have come to try and detain me. I also see you brought some help and they all have tasers out. Why have you not went ahead and just shoot me?

Easy Hans! I know you do not want to come along peaceful like so I will ask this once. You are under arrest for the crimes of selling and distributing weapons of mass destruction and death and the rape of several females around the world. Yes Han's we found your date from last night she will live. And I will also be there to testify against you.

Oh how touching! Enough talk Han's you coming or not?

Well I will say Not and with that said he does a very fast spin kick and Linda blocks it with her rock hard butt muscles. She does a quick snap kick that connects with his left wrist and a gasp in pain as his hand pops open and he momentarily holds it. He says Bitch that will cost you dearly.

Come on Little man talk is cheap. He ups the ante and pulls a long slim looking knife out and Linda says you just made a mistake. She then pulls the tanto and settles in a Japanese knife fighting stance and Hans is slightly puzzled.

So bitch you want me to gut you eh! He says I will even do it fast so you will have little pain. Linda just stands there ready. Hans advances and lunges and Linda with a quick circle parry drives his blade away from her. She ripostes his and she is there with hers and the blades clang against each other as sparks fly from Han's blade.

She circle around and she shifts her blade to a point up position and tests his abilities. He after a few minutes of feints and stabs at and a few cuts. She has his measure. He is good with a blade but does not have the mental training for it. She centers herself and sets in her stance and shifts her blade again back to point down.

Then he lunges and he goes into a fury of moves, very fast and desperate moves. She quickly blocks or parry's all that he had to offer. Then she see's an opening and slices the outside of his forearm. He hisses in pain and says bitch you will die because of that.

You talk too much and she lashes out with her right foot and connects with his balls and crushes them. He lets go and drops the knife and his eyes some what go bug eyed and them he falls to the ground holding his family jewels with his hands.

Hamish looks at his wife and says to her remind me to never get in an argument with you. Well you I love and I love our sex life I would not kick you in our family jewels. But please sedate him and let's get him out of here.

The club manager come up with a Disc case and says here is the security disc for the last few nights and it also has that fantastic fight in it. Why thank you. I will let the base commander know how much you have cooperated with us and also the local police. Why thank you mame.

Hamish and Linda grab Han's and hoist him up and sort of Fireman's carry him out and once inside the SUV he gets about ten plastic cuffs on him.

They get him to the base hospitable and while the doctors check him out Linda goes to check on the one young lady Hans had been so brutal to. She is awake when Linda comes in and says Hello Sergeant How are you doing?

The young lady answers I have been better mame! Please call me Linda and you are? My name is Molly Delohna I am a Technical Sergeant in Base Finance section.

Finance huh well I could use you in my outfit.

I have already done some of the back ground check and you have no family and you have what I call a very good record. Your EPR's are always top rated and your supervisors have nothing but the highest praise.

So Molly asks! Who are you? Well young lady I am you ticket out of here and it was a branch of our Gov't that found you. They acted on my orders to bring you here.

That creep Hans somebody promised me a good time with lots of beer and dancing. But I feel so sick.

That is because he drugged you. Like he did me once. I was on assignment to get some information from him and he gave me some of the same drug.

Only its effects on me were different. Needless to say I am a High level member of the Justice Department now and I have made arrangements for you to be transferred to my command in the states as soon as you are well enough. You will be assigned to my finance office to help with the budget I will get.

Wow This is pretty fantastic! Well Molly what do you say? I want it bad. That is why I have been going to school to be a member of the Spy game of sorts. Well I am not really a spy. I am a special Investigator and Director for the Justice Department and My name is Linda King.

Yes mame! All right Tech Sergeant Delohna get some rest and get better. The orders will be cut within the next few days and you will be testifying against Han's in the states as will I and several other lady's. But these charge are Minor compared to the ones I have filed against him. What are those If I may ask? I know you have the clearance to know that and your clearance will get raised as soon as you report for duty. But he will be tried for the sale and distribution of chemical warfare weapons of mass destruction and death along with Radiation poisoning as well.

We have it all well documented. My team and I caught up with him at his favorite night club and I had a little hand to hand combat with himself. He lost!

Get well Molly and call me Linda. Ok Linda see you soon. Linda walks out and heads down stairs and see's that Han's is all set to go. He is still out and the doctors have given him a better sedative and he will be out for several hours now.

They get back to the runway and the Lear jet is gone but there is a C-141 waiting there to take them back across the Atlantic. They load the SUV and take Hans out and strap him in a small cell for prisoners and get seated themselves. After their airborne and going steady Linda calls Alex and says we are on that way back and I have a treat for you. We got him and the club Manager caught it all on his security disc and he gave it to me. So he resisted arrest. Yes he did and I used a lot of restraint on catching him. Otherwise I would have just shot him. I wish I could have done that over the years to a lot of my captures but I have to play by the rules. I know Alex Just venting that's all. See you at the debriefing. After about an hour Linda get the Lap top from Hamish and writes her report.

About two hours later she hands it back and says everybody need to add to that report. Then afterwards I will get some sleep.

I am with on that Luv. She gets her Satellite phone out and contacts the base saying we have a high priority prisoner coming and we need the next cell put up. And call the doctor on this one he may have fun with this one.

Several hours later they land and Agent Harris and Alex are there to help with everything. Alex says you and your team need ninty six hours of down time so go home and relax and come back after four days all right Director!

Linda says you will get no argument from me. But who is going to run this zoo while I am away. Alex points to Harris and says. He will. Linda says Harris you mess up my office I will wring your neck. Then she says I know you will do a good job take care.

They get to Linda's apt and there is a note from her mother saying that Jake is with her for the next week. So Have fun! Linda peels out of her Black skin tight cloths and is standing there naked and says to Hamish Get yours off Husband I want some loving and I want it now. Hamish quickly removes his and they are having wild sex standing right there.

Then they hit the shower and get cleaned up and get in bed and for the next several hours Linda and her husband are of one mind and soul.

 Epilogue

Those four days goes by fast and on the next day Linda and Hamish have already ran six miles and worked out in the weight room and eaten a hearty breakfast. Both have dressed in dark slacks and Hamish has put on a dress shirt and a good suit coat Linda has on her usual dark sleeveless tight shirt and a black jacket as well. They get to the office at six a.m.

It appears the paper work is done from the day before and the office looks good. She muses that Harris is a good man for Alex.

Both of them go over reports on the disposition of their prisoners and find that Alex has had them moved to a Maximum security facility just for those type of prisoners. She and Hamish head out and see how the compound is coming along. She see's that there is a small maintenance area set up for the vehicles.

Later that day Alex calls and says I am having a cook out at my place tonight and it is informal I want to congratulate you on a job well done. Thanks Alex Linda replies, It was a team effort. They will all get some time off from me when I can get it to them.

Good and soon the trial will take place but not for another couple of months and that means you and Hamish will have a proper honeymoon. Well will let you know when ok. Ok be over here tonight at six P.M. All right Alex. The rest of the day goes by smoothly and Jenny and Fiona both come in with smiles on their faces.

So how are you two love birds doing Linda asks. Oh we are just being friends like you and I were Jenny says, But there is nothing wrong with having some fun. No my good friend there is not.

Hamish says to Fiona You having fun Fiona? I sure am and thanks for asking my friend, That's why I am here to keep my friends happy! Jenny says speaking of which Did Alex call you yet. About what!

Dinner tonight at his place. Oh yea we got the invite. He said casual. Which means we wear clothing. Linda smiles I do not mind It is Alex he is a friend and our boss.

The day goes well and they head off a small disaster by sending in a squad of marines and five of their agents to a small little place in Texas and they take down a Taliban cell that became active. All were taken alive and poison teeth were removed. When Linda received the call from the lead Agent she said to her well done and I want all the Marines there to have a commendation out of this. No problem will do Agent Sandy Johansson replies.

That night at Alex's house they are all sitting around the large table out back and dinner hand been consumed a while back and everything cleared away. Alex says Jenny I think it is time we told your former lover and good friend the whole truth! Linda looks at Jenny and Alex with eyes as big as can be and says what is the meaning of this?

Well Linda Jenny says! All those years in the Air Force as a damn good Officer I was so proud of you and when I got my position in with Military Intelligence I thought of you.

You answered all those questions right and then I saw you on vacation at the nudist resort. Well that was planned. I was going to ask you to join up with me in Military Intelligence but it seems you just wanted to do your time and get out. You were right on that Jenny But continue this is getting Interesting. So I went back to my superiors and asked if there was a way we might still be able to get you back into the fold. My commander at the time was a woman and she is still a lesbian.

She really wanted to help you so she put a call into Alex who she had known from years long past. Alex said I will try to lure her in and hire her.

Alex then said I need to finish this now Jenny sure boss. Well Linda when I got the call to hire you I went ahead and started to back ground check and that was the day you got out of the service. I arranged for you to get the only job you could get.

Why you little, Vie spoke up and said now Linda Just listen please I knew this as well. Okay! Alex continues and says I made sure you had a decent wage and stuff so you could live. Then I placed the advertisement on Private investigators needed.

Believe me I got had gotten several calls on that and I did look them over but all would not have made the cut so I sent them to a different source. It was aimed at you and when you sent your resume in and we meet, I wanted to higher you on the spot. Of course I never knew that it would turn into this.

Well if does not beat all. I love you guys and she holds Hamish's hands and says well let catch all the damn terrorists in the world and put them away. My thinking to Alex says.

A few months later after Linda and Hamish spend two who weeks on his friend private island totally alone a doing nothing but nude sunbathing and making love at every opportunity. They come back all recharged and the trail starts for Han's and his two Taliban associates. The initial charges of date rape and assault will be added later. But the world court hears and see's all the evidence of the chemicals and the extreme radiation hazard that have been filed as exhibits for the prosecution.

After all the charges are read and the jury goes out. It comes back one hour later and the verdict is guilty and the penalty is death any means the guilty want. Han's says just shot me in the head and I want that bitch Linda to do it. The two Taliban say we wish to be purified in pain.

Linda says as much as I hate you Han's I just cannot kill you in cold blood like that. Take the rifle squad I will watch if you want. I expected as much from you Linda King of the Justice Department. Well at least I have tasted pleasure from your flesh Linda King. Yes you did but it was not pleasure to me and the drug you gave me made me violently sick. Laughing! I was hoping for more. Did you ever find the other one I drugged down there? Yes she was the other agent there to get information. Oh and By the way I did get the information Those Jammers never worked on my bugs I had. So you will get what you deserve and the world will be a slightly better place to live.

Linda and Hamish go home that night and watch several reruns of Benny Hill and then go to bed very tired.

Later that night the phone rings and Alex says we have another problem!

About the Author

$\mathcal{L}$ayne Landis lives in a small house north of Indianapolis Indiana with his two male cats Stitch and Hamish. He was medically retired for the Air Force in 1999 and has worked in the IT filed and security and vehicle repair. For most of his adult life he has enjoyed Many Role playing table tops games and loves to cook and write.